The Faded Rainbow

A Novel

The Faded Rainbow

Gourahari Das

Translated by
Manoranjan Mishra

Black Eagle Books
2022

Black Eagle Books
USA address:
7464 Wisdom Lane
Dublin, OH 43016

India address:
E/312, Trident Galaxy, Kalinga Nagar,
Bhubaneswar-751003, Odisha, India

E-mail: info@blackeaglebooks.org
Website: www.blackeaglebooks.org

First International Edition Published by
Black Eagle Books, 2022

THE FADED RAINBOW
by **Gourahari Das**
Translated by **Manoranjan Mishra**

Cover: **Tanuj Mallik**
Interior Design: Ezy's Publication

ISBN- 978-1-64560-254-5 (Paperback)
Library of Congress Control Number: 2022932365

Printed in the United States of America

Dedicated To
Dr. Sanghamitra Bhanja
Dr. Sisir Behera
And
Dr. Chinmaya Sahu
Three rising stars in the field of
Odia Literature and Criticism

Gourahari Das
Vasant Panchami, 2022
Bhubaneswar, India

Introduction

Gourahari Das's novel *The Faded Rainbow* is an English translation of his Odia novel *Chhayasoudhara Abasesha* first published in 1996. The protagonist of the novel is Minu. The novel centres round her troubled childhood consequent upon the death of her father, her youthful hopes and aspirations, the crumbling of those hopes, the nastiness of the village elders, her unsuccessful marriage, her adventures in a brothel at Calcutta, and finally her act of nobility and consequential death. The writer mentions, "I discovered Minu from the pages of a newspaper and lifted her from there. Minu Dey, a prostitute living in a brothel, had to undergo untold miseries in her attempt to free a young lady, before she could be forcefully inducted into the tainted profession" (Introduction, Panchaparva).

A carefree, tomboyish and venturous Minu spends much of her childhood days under the care of her maternal grandmother. When she is eleven, her father passes away. This sudden demise forces her to abandon her grandmother's place and live with her widowed mother. Minu matriculates from the village school, but not without facing the hurdles that normally obstruct the path of the ambitious poor. It is when she is barely fifteen that she develops a strange fascination for the revival of the village drama rehearsal hall, in which her father had once played a pivotal role. She somehow impresses her mother to allow her to take the lead. With necessary support coming from Gangadhar Sir, Kirtan, Sura, Sukadeb, Tima and Karuni, the drama troupe is revived. The villagers, however, spare no time, to sully their characters. How can they tolerate when a young girl confronts the challenges of life and moves ahead with her own mission in mind?

The sudden death of her mother comes as a bolt from the blue. In quest for a new life, she agrees to marry the person selected by her cunning and malicious uncle, who deviously plans to get rid of her and take possession of the property of her share. Damodar, her aged and impotent husband, fails to satisfy her physically but is successful in shifting the blame on her. He gets it announced that Minu is a spirit and arranges exorcists to drive the spirit away. Unable to put up with the ignominy of being called a spirit, the disgrace of being falsely branded a barren woman, and the tortures inflicted by the exorcists, she runs away from home one night. She is rescued by the police. Instead of sending her to a destitute home as promised, the inspector of the local police station sends her to a brothel.

Param Mondal, a pimp with the brothel, deceives a poor girl named Arundhati on pretext of giving her jobs and leaves her in the brothel. The unwillingness of the poor girl to accept the trade, her addressing Minu as 'Maa' and her desperate pleas to help her escape, move Minu. She ensures her release but is finally stabbed by Munsif Mian, the owner of the brothel.

Minu's death brings an end to her contemptuous, debased and sorrowful existence but the reader is left wondering, "Isn't she more sinned against than sinning?"

Translator's Note

The Faded Rainbow is the English translation of Gourahari Das's novel *Chhayasoudhara Abasesha*. The Odia novel, published in 1996, was the writer's maiden attempt at the genre.

With more than seventy books to his credit and both the coveted Odisha Sahitya Akademi and Central Sahitya Akademi awards in his kitty, the writer has carved a niche for himself. A multifaceted personality, Mr. Das has penned novels, short stories, travelogues, vignettes, plays and poems. Besides, he has translated books into Odia too.

The Faded Rainbow offers multiple interpretations to the readers. It is no doubt a study in feminism. It can also be interpreted as a quest for self by its female protagonist, Minu. Her attempts to lend meaning to her otherwise frustrated, meaningless and gloomy existence can be another way of looking at it.

On the occasion of the publication of the novel, I express my deep sense of gratitude to Mr. Das for reposing faith in me and permitting me to go ahead with the task.

I thank Mr. R. P. Samal for going through the manuscript and suggesting vital inputs, thereby increasing the readability of the text.

A special word of thanks to Mr. Satya Patnaik, Director, Black Eagle Books, USA for readily accepting the manuscript for publication. I wish the reader's a pleasant reading.

- **Manoranjan Mishra**

Startled, Minu got up from sleep and sat on the bed. Who called her by her name and why? She dragged her reluctant feet to open the door and looked outside. She craned her neck and examined both sides of the window. There was nobody anywhere. Then who called by her name and what for?

She returned to bed and tried to catch some sleep. The evening was yet to come for the street lights to be illuminated. The flower seller was yet to arrive. She could relax a little longer. She closed her eyes to go to sleep. But sleep eluded her. Once sleep is broken, it is difficult to get back into it.

Again and once again…she felt as if someone was calling her by her name. This time the voice was easy to perceive as if coming from somewhere very nearby.

Who was calling her and why? What work could one have with her?

She failed to relapse into sleep. This sleeplessness often distressed her. On certain nights, it eluded her till dawn. No matter how much she tried, sleep refused to come. All her desperate efforts would go in vain. On some days, she would feel sleepy early in the evening, and then it was too difficult to resist.

She felt as if two or three people were hurriedly heading towards her room. She could hear the dragging of their footsteps both on the staircase and on the verandah. Who were they? Anxiety momentarily disturbed her peace of mind. Why should she be worried? They must be some shameless customers arriving before the onset of evening. She was least interested in them. Suddenly the unpleasant incidents of her past returned to her mind, disturbing her.

She moved closer to the window. She untied the knot on her chignon. The tresses of hair covered her ears, eyes and nose before reaching her knees. She lovingly ran her fingers through her hair and brought the lock to the front. She took a comb and sat doing her hair, while continuing to glance through the window.

Minu often felt nostalgic while arranging and rearranging her hair. Despite the best of her efforts, she was not able to shut the door of her mind on the events of the past. The memories would constantly return and knock on the door. There was no respite from them.

Leaving the comb on the bed, she soothingly wiped her forehead and face and looked at her open palms just as one looks at the pages of an open book. The lines there criss-crossed and ran like courses of rivers and mountains. Below some deep lines ran a number of indistinct ones. These indistinct and blurred lines that look like footprints of crabs on sand are believed to be controlling man's fate.

When Minu was a child, the astrologer of her uncle's village had read her horoscope and said, "She will spend her days in great luxury. She is blessed. Her luck dictates that she will live in grandeur like a queen…a queen, do you understand?"

Minu laughed at the thought. The system of kings had been abolished long ago. How could queens exist without kings? The palaces had turned dilapidated without necessary repairs. Roots of banyan and peepul trees had spread all over the inner chambers. Bricks and stones had fallen off the boundary walls, layer of lime-plaster had peeled off from the walls. How could she become a queen when there was no possibility of a new king ascending the throne? She knew this was a deliberate lie told by the astrologer to make her happy.

Even though the much revered astrologer had cooked up a lie that day, he was treated to a sumptuous lunch besides being adequately remunerated.

A gust of wind blew in through the window from the direction of the sea. Minu again felt as if someone called by her name and suddenly disappeared. Who was it? Leaning on the window she looked downwards but found none. The deserted road during the evening deepened her loneliness.

Things had taken a strange turn over the last few days. She would often get up in the middle of her afternoon siesta. While talking to someone, she would frequently go absent-minded. The arrival of patches of cloud in the sky made her gloomy. She often felt as if a small girl called her and invited her to play games. "Come, let's play games. Let's roam around the mango grove. Is it the time to lie in bed?" Minu would point at her and say, "Don't shout so loudly ! Let me escape through the back door. Wait for me for some time."

Minu would reminisce the days of her childhood.

Slowly and carefully, Minu would try to escape through the back door, carrying some salt and chilly in one hand, and holding the corner of the frock in the other. The door-hinges would produce a squeaky noise. Her heart would start pounding heavily. Grandmother would shout from inside, "Who is it? Is it you, Minu? You shrewd tomboy, you are going out once again in this heat ! It's so hot outside that even birds and beasts have returned to their nests to take rest, you are trying to go out at such an hour ! Let me know where you want to go."

Her friend would get an inkling of Minu's misfortune. Without waiting for her anymore, she would run away to spend the time in the lap of the mango grove.

Minu would reluctantly step back into home. Grandmother, while securing the door would say, "Dare you leave the house again, my blows will turn your back red."

Minu would get angry with herself for her failure. She would be terribly angry with her grandmother too. "Oh, what a tartar !"Unable to express her frustration, she would be left grinding her teeth only. She would imagine the fun and frolic of her friends in the mango grove. Although in confinement, she would be making a count of the number of mangoes each of her friends would have plucked by then and the number of times they would have braced success or failure in their attempts. Her mouth would water at the thought of the luscious mangoes.

Outside the window the afternoon sunshine would keep receding, while inside Minu's tears would be drying up. She would be seething in anger remembering her friends. Would the sky have fallen down if they had not come to the groves today?

While she would be seething in anger and frustration, her friend Malati would arrive in the evening to gift her a mango. Minu would discard it and scoot. To hell with friends and mangoes ! To hell with games and assembly of friends ! She hardly needed their company if they failed to empathize.

However, the anger, the emotional outburst and the restrictions hardly mattered the next day. By the time grandmother searched for her after the cooking and other chores were over, Minu would have given her the slip. "Where has the naughty girl disappeared? Who has she gone with?" She would be left wondering.

With her tomboyish trick, Minu would be roaming in the mango groves in the company of her friends. Sitting on a sand heap in the shade of some trees she would be munching mangoes gladly.

Grandmother would decide to secure the door from outside the next day and fasten it with a shackle clip. Otherwise, she would never be able to exercise any restraint on that tomboy.

Tomboy ! Tomboy !

Oh, how many times Minu heard this abusive word being uttered ! It made her blood boil. As if someone had tattooed this word in her heart or on her forehead with a bone-pen and blood-ink !

When she was a child, she hardly gave this abuse a damn. When someone called her tomboy, she would only flash a delightful smile. She would stick out her tongue in reply to the teasing and rush at the teaser raising her hand in an attacking gesture.

Only after she had grown up, she understood the cruelty of this abusive word. She was forbidden from climbing trees and warned against going for a swim, besides being debarred from loitering with her friends in the village streets at odd hours.

Since then, she was reprimanded quite frequently. Each step of her was monitored by others in the family. Each time she expressed her desire to do something she would get a big 'no' in response. Chains of discipline shackled her feet; heaps of advice curtailed her freedom.

Minu did not like to be confined to the four walls. She felt breathless and stifled inside. She would desperately wish to run out into the open to respond to the attraction of the mango trees laden with blossoms, the champak tree inside the temple precincts overflowing with its fragrance, the celebration of *Dolapurnami*, the orchestra, and illumination of marriage processions. Is it possible to resist one's temptation to such attractions?

More importantly, she found the practice sessions of plays in the Rehearsal Hall in preparation for the public performances irresistible.

That Rehearsal Hall ! How it ensnared Minu ! It compelled her to drop her favourite pastime of playing *dalmankudi* with her friends. The fastenings of its net were too intricate for Minu to escape from.

She was only eleven when it all happened.

That year, the *Dolapurnami* celebrations continued for two days. Suddenly, information reached from her village that her father had passed away. The moment her grandmother got the message, she cried so horrendously beating her hand on earth that the whole road leading to the nearby pond shuddered. When the neighbours heard that wailing, they rushed in and surrounded the bereaved. Within minutes, the village street got crowded like a market place. Minu realized that the person who at times visited her with sweets and dolls, who carried her on his shoulders around the village, who displayed love by rubbing his nose on hers, who asked her frequently if the maternal uncle's village was better or their own village, and who danced happily when Minu answered that their own village was much better, had departed for the other world, leaving her behind. The person who sang "*Itikili mitikili phutigala kaincha*" and "*Aa jahnamamu saraga sashi*" in his hoarse voice, and the person who willingly played a four footed horse on her demand, had left this world forever. He had become invisible amidst the sun and the darkness. He would not return to this earth any more. Grandmother helped Minu change into a new frock. However, Minu didn't do her hair. Grandmother dragged her to her lap and said, "My poor child ! How sad it is that you have become fatherless at this tender age." In the midst of wailing, she dispatched her to her father's place with her maternal uncle.

Minu's father departed from the world after he had made a brief appearance, like an evening star. He disappeared before Minu could experience parental love by basking in his affection. Her mother's bangles had to be broken; the vermilion mark on her forehead had to be wiped away. A woman who was enjoying a blissful married life suddenly turned a helpless widow.

With the sudden demise of her father, many other relationships also took to sudden burial. When an old building collapses bricks, stones, tender branches of banyan and peepul trees, iron shackles and hinges on the doors get buried in the debris. In the same way, all the links with the maternal uncle's family and the friends in that village were snapped. No doubt, Minu was saddened by her father's untimely death, but what saddened her more was the snapping of ties with her friends. While leaving the village, she felt as if she was leaving half of her being there and carrying the rest to her own village. All memories of childhood and adolescence dragged her back by holding her little finger, asking her not to go away. She floated them in her tears for one last time before leave-taking from the place.

Someone knocked at the door. Minu got up from the bed and opened it. The florist was standing with a packet of flowers. Minu asked him to leave it on the table.

The fragrance of champak flower wafted all through the room. Minu opened the door and windows. She took out two incense sticks and lighted them. Let the room be cleansed of all the filth. Half-burnt cigarettes and dried drops of wine lying on the floor, the offensively unpleasant odour of sweat and saliva on her body would make her sick. She would feel like throwing up. However, there was no escape for her from these. She had to learn how to live with such terrible stench. These malodors were supposed to be a part of her everyday life. Had it been for a day or two, she would have managed by covering her nose but this was different. The malodor of sweat, wine, cigarette smoke, cannabis and the accompanying indecent talk no longer appeared out of place. She had got used to it all.

Had Minu ever imagined that her life would be confined to the four walls of a filthy room like this? Had she ever thought that her dream of having a family and a husband would be shattered in a day or two? Had she ever envisaged that she would live the rest of her life with the slur of being called an evil spirit?

How disgusting ! Was she an evil spirit?

She was an evil spirit who sucked blood from tender

children. Whether she saw a pretty small child or a strong young man, she would suck their blood within no time using a straw or with the corner of her saree. The person whose blood the witch drank was sure to die within a few weeks. There was no way one could save himself from such an evil spirit.

It was believed that during the fortnight of *krishnapaksha* and on no-moon night, the witch roamed around the cremation ground. With her legs pointed upwards and head pointed downwards, she gobbled up filth there. Before leaving home, she would render her husband unconscious by chanting some *mantras*. On return she would bring him back to consciousness by chanting the revival *mantra*. Anything that met her eyes, whether wood or bamboo, would catch fire, live trees would wither in no time, and if a human being saw her, he was sure to be shocked and go unconscious.

Such disparaging remarks would bang Minu in her tender mind like bricks and stones. She would bleed. She would try to hide her face in the corner of her saree but in vain. At home, she was treated with disdain; outside, people treated her with the greatest contempt. She hardly knew where to get solace from.

Those days of misfortune ushered in Minu's life much later.

After the death of her father, Minu came back home. Although she was fourteen she had to take care of her widowed mother. During leisure time she would go to the drama rehearsal hall.

Why did she spend time at the rehearsal hall?

Was it wise on the part of a fourteen year old girl to shamelessly spend her time there?

Had her mother become shameless to allow her

daughter to go there? It's good that her father had passed away. Why should he have been alive to partake in such disgrace?

Just as handful of paddy sizzle into parched-rice when heated, gossips about Minu spread among the villagers like wildfire. Whether at the bathing ghat, near the altar of the village deity under the banyan tree or on the way to school, gossips went on unabated.

Her female friends avoided her while the boys would wink and try to get close. Such uninvited gestures of the boys annoyed her. She would wish to land blows on the loafer boys. However, she could never say anything to anyone. She only tried to get used to such hostile circumstances.

Darkness had descended. Minu switched on the lights. It was Shiva *Chaturdashi*, a day dedicated to the worship of Lord Shiva. She had undertaken a fast. When it grew darker, she would go to the temple at the end of the street. She would prayerfully fall at the feet of the Lord and return. She would neither go to anyone nor allow anyone to her room so that she could use the evening and the night all by herself.

Memories of the village school flashed before her eyes. She brought to her mind the events associated with Deba Sir, the teacher who was expelled from Rampur, defamed and disgraced, for no fault of his. Neither could Minu say anything in his defence nor could Deba Sir explain anything to prove his innocence. He rather said, "Minu, Don't worry about all this. No one can be held guilty. I blame my fate. I have done my duty. If you respect me, study as much as you can. Do not give in to disappointment. The road to a successful future is very long. There is hardly any time to waste".

Really, the road is very long. That road never ends.

One keeps on searching for the destination throughout one's life but the journey hardly ends. Deba Sir had told the truth. The tall and fair complexioned young man was a man of wisdom, although irritable. Why did he bid goodbye to her village disgracefully? What sort of relationship did he share with her?

Minu heaved a sigh. She picked up the pillow and pressed it to her lap. She held back her tears from streaming down. Do teardrops give in to the bondage of consolations and comforting?

Rivers and ponds kept drying up but Minu's tears continued to flow.

Her matriculation examination was only a month away. After father's demise, she marked a change in the behavior of her uncle. It was good that she was with her maternal uncle earlier. The continuous abuses of uncle and aunt would hardly reach Madhupur.

Her paternal uncle, who was dissatisfied with the division of property, blamed Minu's father for all the troubles that he faced. He would rub salt on their wounds by continuously pointing out, 'One who creates trouble for others has his children in trouble.' Minu was not a child anymore; she understood clearly what her uncle had in mind. She didn't protest keeping her mother's pleadings in mind.

If she failed to fill-up forms in time, she wouldn't be allowed to appear at the final examination. Who could she tell this? Minu's mother knew everything but was helpless. Minu didn't wish to create further trouble for her. She would rather not take the examination. This was perhaps the only option.

The month of March had arrived. New leaves had sprouted on trees. Minu was returning from school carrying her books. No classes were to be held from the next day. Those who were going to write the final examination had to stay at home and prepare for it. Those who weren't going to write it also had to stay at home. Minu felt a vacuum inside her heart. Her education was a means of living life. It was a means of spending seven hours at school. She spent her time well amidst friends. What would she do from tomorrow? On what pretext would she come out?

Deba Sir called out loudly from behind, "Minu, listen".

Minu went to Deba Sir. He was a good and dedicated teacher. When he taught lessons, he would often find himself lost in the subject. He would share his joys and sorrows with the students. During leisure he would narrate amusing stories.

That Deba Sir was calling Minu to him. What for? The pond side was deserted. The school was over. Almost everybody had left for home. Minu went near him and stood in front of him, with downcast eyes.

Deba Sir said, "Minu, you are like my younger sister. She is also going to write the matriculation examination this year. But, you are better than her in studies".

What answer should she give? She stood with downcast eyes. The sooner she got opportunity to escape, the better.

Deba Sir said, "I know, you must be having some problems. Therefore, you haven't filled up forms for the final examination. I have paid for you. Go and put your signature on the form. Concentrate on your studies. You have many responsibilities to shoulder".

Minu didn't know what to say. She had become wet with perspiration. She recoiled into herself just as a turtle drags its neck and legs inside the protective cover at the sight of danger. Deba Sir had paid the required fees. She could now take the examination ! Her studies wouldn't suffer !

She mustered up courage and said, "But...why?"

"You can return the amount whenever you want. I haven't donated the amount to you. I have only lent it," said Deba Sir and went away.

The problem concerning exam fees was solved but another problem cropped up. Gossips took to wings in the entire school. "Deba Sir paid fees for Minu. He'll also pay for her college education. He loves her. He'll marry her."

"Loves me? What sort of word is that? What does it mean?" Minu didn't know the meaning of the word till that day. Deba Sir taught her at school, he had helped her in her need. She was thankful to him for that. Why should this 'love' trespass in between? Where did Deba Sir get it from? She, on her part, didn't love anyone. If someone helped the other, should it be called a case of love?

It hardly mattered whether Minu loved someone or not. Her body and beauty had adequately blossomed to be worthy of being loved. They had become so fertile that scandals could easily grow and spread their wings among the rumour-mongers. Minu learnt about it later in her life. But, was there anything she could do other than shedding tears?

The day she understood the implications of Deba Sir's action, the distinctive feature of the teacher illuminated her mind. What difficulties he had to face as he was falsely implicated for his efforts to help a helpless girl ! What was his fault? Was it a sin to render help to a helpless girl? "Can't a young girl be someone's sister or daughter? Can't the relationship between two young people be a pious one? Can't two people harbor any relationship except one that fosters physical intimacy? Why does the society examine such relationships only under the prism of meanness?"

It would have been better if she had loved the teacher. Had she done that, the remaining years of her life wouldn't have been burnt down to ashes. Her youth and life wouldn't have ended in smoke.

Deba Sir, however, didn't raise any objections; he didn't bother to answer anyone. He left fondly cherishing a hope in his heart. He hoped that Minu would surely be educated. She would create a space for her in the society. That would silence all the gossip-mongers and bring all condemnations to rest.

How spineless his hope was ! A sob that caused a convulsive gasp was restless to come out violently tearing her apart. Such things happened only in the improbable accounts of stories and fables. For example, a poor person who had gone without food for two days would be treated to a sumptuous meal on the third day. A poor man would suddenly become rich. A prince would marry a pauper's daughter and carry her to the palace. But real life is different from the life that the tales tell. Even millions of stories could have no visible impact on the course of life. Deba Sir's hopes had been crushed. His dreams had been shattered. Minu wanted to say that the person whose hopes were belied felt as much heartbroken as the person on whom his hopes rested. It's true that one of Deba Sir's dreams had been shattered but nobody bothered that Minu's entire life had been afflicted with shame and suffering.

Was it life or a heart full of unfulfilled wishes? Or a prolonged cry of despair !

After that incident, Minu turned into 'an object of ridicule' for the entire village. She became the topic of all arguments and counter arguments. In the otherwise sleepy mofussil school Minu's existence brought a fresh wave of excitement. Minu could experience this herself. Although she condemned herself for her misfortune, she couldn't gather enough courage to raise a voice of protest. She was afraid that her protest might encourage them to be more savage in their attack.

Since the form fill-up was over, she no more needed to go to school. Her relationship with school was going to end after the examinations were over.

In the darkness of night, Minu would hold on to her mother and cry. She always wanted to ask her mother why they had so many sorrows in life. What had she done to deserve so much ridicule and so much contempt?

Her mother wished to give her grown up child the protection she needed. Minu would suddenly feel like a small child inside her mother's affectionate arms. How she wished to have remained a small child all through her life, in which case, she wouldn't have become the easy victim of abuses and mockery of the villagers.

In that darkness, Minu would feel as if her mother caressed her, went on planting kisses one after another on her forehead and caressed her long hair lovingly.

Minu cried out, "Mother…O my dear mother". Her eyes welled up in tears. So much love, so much affection, so much concern ! She couldn't even return her love. The debts remained unpaid.

Minu's life was no better than that of a cursed debtor. She could never pay off anyone's debt. She couldn't return anyone's love. She provided pleasure to those who never ever contributed to her happiness. What a cursed life she had !

Minu bent down to shut the windows. She would leave the door unfastened and go to the temple. On her return she would quietly switch off all lights and lie down on bed for sleep to come.

A young man passing by her window whistled on seeing Minu. He looked up at her shouting, "Hey…you… the queen of my hearts !" Closing the doors with a thud and covering her face with her palms, she sat on the bed feeling agonized. A surge of shame, anger and hate inflamed her whole being.

Moments later she cooled down and came to terms with the reality. How could the young man be faulted? Whether her heart accepted it or not, she was a prostitute. It was her duty to satisfy the appetite of her customers. To be attracted by customers spoke volumes of her being worthy of her profession, it was an insignia of appreciation. A praise that should make her pleased, not agitated.

She knew the young man. For the last several days, she had spotted him passing by that lane. His eyes reflected an insatiate hunger. As if he would swallow the whole of her ! Even hunger in the eyes of an eagle would not radiate so much of appetite.

She closed the door and came downstairs. Night had deepened. The ill-famed lanes were less crowded that night. Why should someone be a sinner by visiting a prostitute on a holy day like Shiva *Chaturdashi*. It was a day earmarked to earn piety. Sins could be earned any other day. Today, they would visit temples with their wives. They would worship Lord Shiva with bel leaves. They would bathe the phallus image in milk and offer coconuts to appease Him.

Piety ! Hadn't Minu earned any piety in her life? Didn't the balance sheet of her life have any trace of piety on it? Was she destined for hell after death? Will her bare body sizzle like a live fish in the frying pan?

Minu wasn't ready to believe that there's something

like hell. If there's hell, elsewhere, what should then the earth be called? Heaven?

Minu would smile at herself in self-ridicule.

The temple was crowded. Minu had put on a cotton saree with a thin border. She didn't need to apply cosmetics that day. When she handed over the garland of champak flowers to the priest, her hands were trembling. What if someone recognized her ! What problems she would have to encounter then ! She pulled the veil further down and handed over the *bhog* basket to the priest. When she raised her right hand to ring the temple bell, the sobs that had accumulated in her chest and the tears that had welled up in her eyes were struggling hard to find a release. Minu held them back in the corners of her saree. The not-so-wide precinct of the small temple was filled with an assortment of smells--burnt out ghee-dabbed wicks, incense sticks, resin, champak flowers and *bel* leaves. Minu breathed in a whiff of this unique aroma. What a divine pleasure !

There was still some more time for the *Mahadeepa* to be raised. Minu pushed a folded note into the donation box and returned with the *bhog* basket.

By the time Minu reached her room, it was ten in the night. Minu found that light in Badadei's room was still on. Badadei never remained awake this late. Only when high ranking government officials or police personnel visited, she was compelled to remain awake. On other occasions, she would retire to her private chamber by nine.

She got down from the rickshaw and had hardly climbed the stairs when Badadei called out to her, "Is it you, Minu?"

Minu replied, "Yes, Badadei."

"Please come and meet me."

Had it been some other day, Minu would have

reached there soon. But today she wasn't interested to hear other's words. From there she asked, "Do you have any urgent business?"

Badadei replied, "Okay, you can go now. I'll talk to you in the morning."

The sea roared intermittently beyond the window. Although surrounded by the darkness of the no-moon night, the waves of the sea shone like the neck of a serpent with a raised hood. Salty and cold breeze blew in from afar.

Minu had hardly slept for two hours when she suddenly got up. As usual, a small girl called out to her by her name. This time her voice came not from beyond the window but right from near the foot of the bed. That voice forced her to sit up. She opened the window and looked out as if searching for someone.

Perhaps the sounds of kettledrums and harmonium floated in through the air. Like hailstones raining down on earth, the two sticks banged on the kettledrums. The excitement on the surface of the drum quivered into music in which the tender sound of the harmonium would rhythmically sink in and swim away.

Minu shut her eyes tight. In that darkness she felt as if the music that she had loved so dearly was floating in from somewhere. The combined music of kettledrums and harmonium floated in, creating a flutter in her heart. Has she ever been able to detach herself from that sweet music? It's the tulsi-grove of her unfulfilled desire, the cactus of disgrace and scandal.

The lighted rehearsal hall flashed in Minu's mind. After she had left the village she heard that her uncle and his followers were planning to raze it to the ground. They carried spades and crowbars with them and demolished the walls. However, they failed to demolish the entire structure. Its pillars grew weaker, the thatched roof was blown away and finally the walls crumbled. However, it couldn't be completely wiped out. In the darkness of night uncle returned from the spot, dazed by the encounter with a ghostly spirit. He announced throughout the village that the rehearsal hall was haunted. It was the spirit which played the harmonium, the *tabla,* the *mridanga* and the flute. It was too dangerous to be in the place.

Minu smiled at the memory. How many accusing tales were woven around her in her lifetime ! She was accused of being a ghost and a spirit that chomped people raw.

She would feel happy at the thought that the rehearsal hall hadn't been wiped out completely from the surface of the earth, although it had been subjected to great contempt. She felt no one had the ability to inflict any harm on it. She had hidden it in her heart and given it space in its lonely corners.

She remembered those days when no one even thought of causing any harm to the hall. Elderly villagers gathered on its verandah after returning from fields in the evening. The village children didn't forget to join them after their afternoon games. They were all eager to know what plays were being rehearsed there.

The year before Minu passed her matriculation, a play was staged in her school on the occasion of Saraswati Puja. Minu played a role for the first time. Despite the disgracing gossips doing rounds about her, everybody liked her performance. She played the role of Urmila, Laxman's wife. Together with Ramachandra, Laxman went on exile to the forest. Laxman's reverence for his elder brother and his dedication to him were re-affirmed. Ramachandra had his dearest wife Sita with him. Before being abducted by Ravan, she stood by him to share the sorrows of exile. What did the grief-stricken Urmila achieve, confined in the lonely corners of the palace? Didn't she bear the brunt of separation for fourteen long years? Was she considered noble the way Sita was? Before leaving for the forests, her husband never asked for her opinion. This was because Laxman was never another person; he was the shadow of Sriram. Minu, through her role-play, skillfully presented the misfortune of being the wife of a shadow. She dedicated her knowledge, mind and heart to her role and garnered enough compassionate tears and sighs for that unfortunate character in Ramayan that day.

The performance was over. Curtains were drawn on the stage. Minu's transformation into Urmila ended there. Everything should have drawn up to a close there. It would have been proper for her if she had erased the make up from her face and lived like Minu only. Strangely, the fifteen day rehearsal and that night's performance on the stage had completely transformed her into another woman. A strange desire to bid goodbye to the immediate present and escape into another fascinating world thrilled her. She didn't prefer one but two worlds to live with in her lifetime.

The temptation of the club was too difficult to resist. Defying mother's refusal to approve, uncle's heart-burning abuses and villagers frowning faces she would arrive in time. Minu wonders today how she could muster so much courage to surmount all such obstacles ! How a daring lady imbued with so many dreams and possibilities could accept the compulsion of living such a cursed life ! Minu herself found the thought difficult to fathom. Those times were different; the courage that permeated through her was different. She did what she thought was right. It hardly mattered if someone supported her or not. She dared the dream of living her life on her own terms.

The moment the rehearsal hall came to her mind, she was reminded of Gangadhar Sir. Kirtan, Sura, Sukadev, Tima and Karuni also flashed before her eyes. The otherwise lifeless club used to bustle with activity with the participation of these people. Wooden swords, tin shields, imitation clothes, harmonium, tabla, kettle drums, *dhols* and ghungroos transported Minu to her second world.

Where were all of them? Minu tried to remember. Gangadhar Sir was no more there. A strange person ! Once he began to play the *dhol,* he would never stop. He would have no knowledge when day dawned. His palms would bleed, the *dhol* might crack, but there would be no end to his playing. Infuriated with anger and helplessness, he would throw the *dhol* away. Let it break, I don't mind ! Then he would rush back home without casting a gaze on others.

Did anyone care for him at home? Did his charming second wife, his son from the first wife or his son's wife care? No one did. Gangadhar Sir was addicted to cannabis; he would spend most of his earnings on this soft drug for euphoric effect. He would hardly mind the household affairs. How would a family run if he played the *dhol* day in and day out? Gangadhar Sir would never disclose the affairs of his home, not even to Minu. Like the inner vacuum in a beautifully adorned *dhol,* his family life was veiled under a close-kept secret. No one needed him at home. He would return from his door to the confines of the rehearsal room. The stray dogs roaming about the streets would rush towards him in the darkness of night. The midnight moon hiding behind patches of clouds would lead him with its dim light like an oil-lamp. On reaching the rehearsal hall, he would collect the musical equipment lying scattered all over—the ghungroos, cymbals, wooden sword, tin shields and his own *dhol*. Stuffing some cannabis into the chillum, he would light it. He would then hold the *dhol* in his lap, as lovingly as a father holding his child, and start playing it slowly. The beating of the fingers would crescendo with the passage of time. Dawn would break. Gangadhar Sir wouldn't stop playing the *dhol*. The sound of the *dhol* would pierce through the stillness of the night and spread everywhere. That was his complaint against the world. That was his explanation. It was not only his dedication but was also his consolation.

Gangadhar Sir never complained against anyone. He had never fostered any hopes of anything in return. Minu thought at times why he frequented the rehearsal room, played the drums and directed the play. Was it his love for plays or his disdain for his family that kept him glued to the rehearsal hall? She had thought of asking him all about it. But Gangadhar Sir's bloodshot eyes, solemn appearance and self-imposed busy schedules didn't give her any opportunity for that.

How she wished she could meet him today ! Would God allow her an opportunity to meet that condemned human being, she would ask him if it was the attraction of the *dhol* that had turned him an ascetic ! How?

No, there's no possibility of finding an answer to her query. Gangadhar Sir had passed away long ago and turned into tender grass at the cremation ground. Did tender grasses answer anyone's queries? Certainly not !

Minu had told him once, "You are the soul of this club.

Without you, it has no existence." Gangadhar Sir had burst into a loud laugh—a laugh loud enough to blow away the old thatched roof.

"No…no, I am not its soul. In fact, you are its soul. You don't realize this today but some day or the other you would certainly understand."

Minu wanted to say that she had, throughout her life, acted as per the instruction of others, she had cried and smiled upon instruction from him. How could such a person become the soul of something? Was soul subservient to anything else? Could it be subjugated? She couldn't say him anything except smiling a satisfying smile.

She had met Gangadhar Sir near the rehearsal hall where the Bhagavad Gita was recited. Mukunda Mohapatra would play the *mridanga* there. Many times during the recital he would go out of tune. In order to cover up his inefficiency, he would abuse the priest who recited the lines.

Gangadhar Mallick would be sitting some distance away from the community centre, disdainfully ostracized. He would receive no invitations to play the *mridanga*. The reason was simple. He was a *harijan,* a low caste untouchable. Hence the sole right to play the *mridanga* rested with Mukunda Mohapatra, irrespective of the mistakes he made. When Mohapatra forgot the measure, the dissatisfied priest would stop the recital and gaze in his direction. Gangadhar Sir, sitting some distance away, would get on his feet and grumble in anger but to no avail.

Minu understood the misery of Gangadhar who despite possessing adequate talent was discarded by the society. This is precisely why she handed over the responsibility of the director to Gangadhar Mallick. There could not have been a better choice.

The day Minu passed matriculation, tears rolled down from her mother's eyes. That day, she did sit beside Minu and caressed her head and back. Fascination for the rehearsal hall had already germinated in Minu's mind by then. Her father and uncle had constructed this rehearsal hall when they were young. With the passage of time, the rehearsal hall came to play the role of a store house of the village deity's property. The temple utensils and firewood were stored there.

It was from her mother that Minu had heard how her father and uncle, together with other young men of the village, organized plays like *Harischandra, Rasaleela and Nala Damayanti*. Her mother was newly married then. During festivities like *Panchudola, Panasankranti* and *Raja*, these plays were staged in front of the deities.

When she talked about the roles that father played on the stage, Mother's withered face would start gleaming. A smile would appear there. She would often exaggerate her praise. Her thin bashful lips and wide eyes trembled. Mother's words would often leave Minu dreaming. One day in the future, she would also feel bashful while talking about someone.

One day Minu told her mother, "Mother, will you please honour a small request of mine?"

Her mother said, "Yes…tell me what it is." Minu said, "A strong and intense bonding bound my father to the rehearsal hall. I want to help it regain its lost glory. I wish to see it throbbing with activity as it was in the past."

Mother bit her tongue in utter disgust as if she had spoken something outlandish. "What strange things this girl always talks about ! After tree-climbing and swimming in the village pond, she now talks about organizing plays !"

"No…never. This simply can't be done. So long as

I'm alive, I can't permit you to shake your limbs and dance with the village young men."

Minu's confidence lay shattered. Her inner being was devastated at her mother's refusal. In the darkness of the night, she would dream of her father's face floating towards her--a smiling face, actor's physique, long, oily hair curling at the back, and sprightly eyes !

On such occasions, the wretchedness of the actor's experiences rushed into her thought as mental images. Thoughts about the relationship that she had as a child years ago resurfaced. She felt as if she comprehended her father's pathetic experiences quite well. She could understand the dreams and determinations of a man opposed to the ways of the world. A strange invisible relationship would take shape with him. There, no one was a father; no one was a daughter either. Life revolved around playing the assigned roles, with make up, stage, songs and dances. She would sit close to the man and ask him, "How are you?"

The man would answer, "I am good."

"Good? Do you call this a life worthy of living?"

The boisterous laughter of the man in response brought her from dreams to reality.

Minu would try to understand the emotions of her mother. She would try to assess the courage of an illiterate woman who left her father's house with an actor and gave her best to manage her family. For a moment, she would leave aside the dreams of reviving the theatre and fall asleep, collecting fragments of the disturbed sleep. But sleep would become elusive as usual.

That actor would come again, sit by her side and ask, "What, already accepted defeat?" Minu would get up, startled. Was she defeated? How? How was she defeated when she hadn't even started anything?

The fire of infatuation for the rehearsal hall would remain burning in her.

It was this infatuation that had engulfed her completely for the last ten years. How could it go away so easily? For those ten years, it was her breath for life. While taking care of its upkeep and purchasing various articles, she often skipped lunch and dinner. She would spend much of her time answering the accusations of the envious and distrustful.

It now became a regular affair with Minu to convince her mother and entreat her for permission. In the meantime, she had got hold of the key to the rehearsal hall, lying in one corner of a casket. She had even gone alone, opened the rusting lock, and inspected the inner space. The moment the door was opened, a bundle of rotten hay fell from the roof. The inside of the hall was dark. Spider-webs spread here and there. Discarded wings of pigeons, droppings of lizards and cockroaches lay scattered all over. Perhaps the hall had been deserted for years. Spider-webs entangled Minu's face. A layer of dust accumulated on her garments. When she closed the door, it produced a loud creak, breaking the silence of the afternoon. Minu locked it quietly and returned home.

While lying for her afternoon siesta, she had a vision of her previous experience in the role of Urmila. In the twinkle of an eye, she became into Urmila of the *Treta Yuga*. The earthly-stage was transformed into the palace of Ayodhya. She was transformed into Urmila, wife of Laxman. What a divine feeling she experienced !

"Had I been a son, you wouldn't have imposed so many restrictions on me," shouted Minu angrily at her mother, "The girls have gone ahead in life. There are many instances of such girls. Sadly, you don't even allow me to participate in a play, that too in our own village. Tell me, what would I do idling at home all the time?"

Her mother was sentimentally hurt that day. While caressing Minu mother had repeated, "You aren't only my daughter; you are my son as well." Repeating this statement of her mother, Minu convinced her and got her consent.

Finally, she handed over the key of the rehearsal hall, but not before placing numerous prohibitive conditions upon her. She had blurted out angrily, "Your father was an actor. She has her actor–father's genes. What else she could be if not an actress?" Minu knew quite well that her mother didn't wish her to be an actress. She handed over the key only because Minu had insisted on getting it. Minu could never blame her mother for her fears and refusals. No mother, who had taken birth, grown up and set up a family under the conditions in which Minu's mother had lived, would have allowed her daughter to become a theatre actress.

Minu invited Gangadhar Sir to work with her. Gangadhar brought Kirtan and Karuni with him. Many works remained to be done. The hall had to be cleaned; some articles given out to village folks had to be collected. The thatched roof had to be newly laid. How could someone sit under a leaking roof? Then, the play was to be selected for the rehearsal to begin.

Minu's apprehensions came to be true. After the rehearsals had stopped, villagers borrowed the harmonium, the *dhol*, the groundsheet and other articles. She became an enemy of the entire village while collecting those back from them. Despite the best of her efforts she failed to retrieve all articles.

A deep sigh escaped through Minu's quaking chest. It was almost dawn. The sea appeared placid. The stars appeared dim. A bird flew around the tree on which it had nested, before flying away into the distance.

The brothel resembled a deserted cremation ground at this hour of the day. The customers had returned. The tired and worn out girls had fallen asleep. It was time for the rule of silence.

Minu opened the door and came out. Here and there on the verandah lay cigarette butts, remnants of betel cones, and stale flowers. Minu lived on the upper floor of the two-storeyed building. A circular staircase, with its base on the ground floor led to her room. Two large halls were there on the ground floor. At times, dances and songs were organized there. Earlier, such programmes were organized quite regularly. No one has enough spare time these days. They all arrived, like hungry diners visiting restaurants, with hunger written all over their faces and ready to gobble up everything within their reach. They would drink a few glasses of wine and arrange their dresses before disappearing.

Minu's eyes were drooping. She felt extremely tired in her body and mind. Since the previous day, she had gone on a fast but she hardly had the desire to eat anything.

Minu climbed down the stairs. After a few hours the place was going to bustle with crowd. Donned in skin-tight georgette dresses or silk saree and blouse, the girls would sit near the railings on the windows, near the doors, or on the roof with their legs outstretched and throw smiling invitations shamelessly. Preparations for another night would begin.

Minu reached the hall on the ground floor. The door was left ajar. It was a big hall. Chandeliers hung from the ceiling. The walls and windows glistened in the morning sun. A groundsheet lay crumpled, with a cushion on it.

There were a few pillows arranged against the wall. Minu walked by them. She had danced on numerous occasions in this hall. Initially she danced here happily, with a desire to attract customers. Then she danced unwillingly, out of compulsion.

In the space between two cushions, a *ghungroo* had got stuck. At the touch of Minu's feet, it twinkled. Minu picked it up with her toes and pushed it away. The *ghungroo* rolled on the cement floor breaking the monotony of silence.

The rehearsal hall was ready with renovation.

Two festivals like *Pana Sankranti* and *Basanti Durga Puja* were to be celebrated one after another. *Chandrasekhar Natya Manch* was going to stage three plays over three nights. Minu had lost her sleep thinking of the preparations. Gangadhar Sir, Kirtan and Karuni worked day and night to make things successful. They had hardly any time on hand.

Gangadhar Sir said, "If the play is based on scriptures, there won't be much demand. Audience will reject it for being old-fashioned. We must include a social story." Kirtan went a step ahead to suggest, "People aren't much interested in social plays either. If there's a blend of suspense and romance, it'll leave an impact." Karuni was the youngest among them all. He placed a proposal: "We should go for one scripture based or historical play, one social play and another detective play. In that case, there would hardly be any objections. We'll get invitations from all."

But where were the resources going to come from? Only 'intent' would not work. Right intent needed right support. Why were the rehearsals not happening for such a long time? Gangadhar Sir seemed to have no answers to this query from Minu. She didn't intend to insult him by asking such questions. Karuni was a small child. What's the use of discussing matters related to money with him? Kirtan had been doing his best. He had been finding it very difficult to get back articles of the rehearsal hall. He was likely to collapse under more pressure.

One day, Minu was sitting on the verandah of the rehearsal hall. The hem of her blue saree spread on the verandah. Her hair lay loose on her back. Her gaze was fixed on the branches of a tree in the distance. Suddenly, Karuni appeared with Suka. Although Minu had heard about him earlier, she had never met him. He lived in another lane although in the same village. He had married two years ago.

Without any formal introduction Sukadeb said, "I have heard about your opera party. Tell me how much money you people require, of course the bare minimum. I'll send the amount. Karuni would not allow me any peace without it. I was on my way to the market. He dragged me here."

Minu looked in the direction of Karuni with a blend of affection and feigned anger. How much the small child was worried about the success of the plans they had made ! She felt delighted to hear what Sukadeb had said. A sense of gratitude bowed her down. She requested him to sit down for some time for Gangadhar Sir to come. He had the required list ready in his mind.

Since that day Sukadeb played the role of a patron of the troupe. He would visit the rehearsal hall once both in the morning and in the evening. He would sit down for some time and watch the rehearsal. He would discuss weal and woe with Gangadhar Sir. He had great fun with Karuni. After some time, he would get up and leave.

Minu was overwhelmed with gratitude, although she never found the right words to express her feelings. From among the stars shining brightly in the distant sky, she would try to identify her father. She felt as if her father showered his blessings on her. Sukadeb reaching her and offering his services must be the consequence of her father's blessings.

The same was the case with Sura and Tima. Sura didn't belong to her village but rather to the neighbouring Baliapal. He was unattractive in look but was gifted with an enchanting voice. At the rehearsal hall, everybody called him 'cuckoo'. Sura had worked for some time in a professional opera troupe. The worsening financial condition of his family and his forced marriage compelled him to return to the village. Otherwise, he would be continuing there till today.

Sura sang so well.

As if the song itself came out dancing of its own in sync with the tune.

He never became tired. He never complained. He was another person crazy about acting. Gangadhar Sir would affectionately call him 'son'.

Tima stood apart from all others in terms of appearance and character. He was so well-known by this name that no one wished to identify him as Krushnamohan, his proper name. His appearance and voice were unquestionably sweet. Fair, tall and healthy—he was the most suitable candidate to play the protagonist. It was as if he was born for the role. No one ever raised any objections to his playing the lead.

The rehearsal hall reverberated with noise now. Just as an insignificant mound transforms itself into a vibrant stage on the night of the performance, the rehearsal hall that had looked like an abandoned cowshed a few months back appeared loveable and vibrant. A blue signboard dominated the entrance. It was the idea of Sura and Karuni. Curtains hung on the doors and windows. The inner walls were adorned with imitation swords and shields to look like palace walls. On the left side, all musical instruments were kept. These included the harmonium, the tabla, the *dhol*, the cymbals, the ghungroos, and the bugle. On the right side, stage-like arrangements had been made. A groundsheet was spread on the floor. From the wooden poles holding the roof hung iron-hooks to hold petromax lights for lighting the stage.

To the right of the rehearsal hall stood the village whereas to the left stretched the vast pond. At its back, there were the mango groves. Beyond the mango groves stood the cashew plantation. Tall coconut trees decorated the pond sides. The rehearsal hall was the first attraction for the visitors to the village. From late in the afternoon till late in the evening, practice performances went on seamlessly. The place kept reverberating with the music of the kettle drum, the harmonium, the ghungroos, and the bugle.

The village elders would sit inside to watch the rehearsals. The children were debarred from entering the hall. They would assemble eagerly outside the windows and peep through the chinks to see what was happening inside. They beseeched Karuni to allow them to stand near the door for a few minutes and watch. Once permitted, they would stand there for hours, until Karuni drove them away.

The members were so deeply engrossed in their job that they would hardly have any idea when day dawned and departed or when evening gave way to night. Their days and nights were spent in fine-tuning their performances and in adding tricks to startle the audience. Their dedication and devotion impelled Minu to forget her hunger and thirst and work dedicatedly towards converting the institution into a self-sustaining one. With the passage of time, the rehearsal hall became her passion and profession.

"Where have those days gone?"

How those intimate experiences disappeared into thin air ! Those days, the verandah of the rehearsal hall seemed like the twenty-two steps of *Srimandir*, its dust as holy as the sand of *Saradhabali* and the surroundings resounding with sounds of musical instruments replicated the atmosphere of *Rathyatra*. It is difficult to believe how time had slipped away so quickly.

Two days before the *Pana Sankranti*, tents were put up in the school field. They had sought the help of five musicians from outside. Plays on three consecutive nights ! It was not child's play. The news had spread through the gossips of children. These children would stop for some time and watch the labourers at work before proceeding to their school. It was but natural that the message took to wings through them.

Until the last moments, Minu had kept a big secret wrapped in her heart. Deliberately, she hadn't let the cat go out of the bag. She suspected that if her mother had whiffs of it, she would never allow her to go ahead with her plans.

Minu herself was the heroine of all the three plays. She was to play Sati in *Dakshyagna*, Rizia in *Rizia Sultan*, and Malati in *Hasa Luha*. She hadn't disclosed this to her mother. She was happy that she had been able to keep such a secret to herself. At the same time, she dreaded her mother's reproach once the secret was out. The combined effect of joy and fear made her absent-minded. She was shivering with anxiety and fearful expectations. She mumbled 'Save me Baba Chandrasekhar' many times during the day.

Sukadeb had no rest. He had completely forgotten about his family and fields. His younger brother would visit him at times during the rehearsal and say, "Brother, there is none to mind the shop. Please come." Sukadeb would say,

"Go…go. I have no time for these mundane affairs." His intense involvement led many a storm to sweep through his family. Minu was no stranger to such developments.

Was there a dearth of critics in the village? Villagers who gathered at the *Palamandap* talked incessantly about the rehearsal hall and the affairs taking place there. The village elders were often heard complaining that Gangadhar Sir had spoiled the village youths. They suspected that Tima's future was going to end in a naught and Karuni was going to pay for his evil associations.

And finally, all discussions would centre round Minu. No…no…she had been the centre of all their discussions from the very beginning. Only at times, they would take a detour and finally come back to dissect her affairs. How wouldn't they? The rehearsal hall existed for generations. Only boys went there for rehearsals. The boys would play the female roles. At times, they invited some actor or actress from other parties to play the female leads. No tomcat, other than Minu, had ever gone to dance among the boys. Forget about dancing, no one even talked freely with the boys.

"She was spoiled from the very beginning. She spent her childhood in her grandparents' village. There she climbed on trees and swam in ponds. She roamed here and there without care. Spare the rod, spoil the child. Aren't there daughters in other families?" Minu's uncle would thus add spice to the gossip of elders.

When the abusive attack of his uncle reached her, she would sit deeply depressed for some time. Perhaps the elders were right. She should tread on the path that society and culture had laid out for girls like her. When such thoughts came to her mind, she would think that she should better pull off the thatched roof of the rehearsal hall, throw away the *dhol* and harmonium, be at home once and for all, and get lost in the kitchen chores.

Yes, Minu should be in the kitchen only. The society wants that all girls should do that. The near and dear ones derive a strange satisfaction the moment they find a girl confined to the kitchen and dealing with smoke and fire. The intense sneezing and coughing that the smoke causes, lends a meaning to the life of girls, they say. Minu is expected to do the same, leaving aside everything else.

Despite such imposing and persuasive thoughts, Minu found it impossible to traverse in that direction. She would find Gangadhar Sir teaching a new tune to Sura. Sura's fingers would be playing on the reeds of the harmonium. Gangadhar Sir himself would be playing the *drum*. Karuni would be doing something or the other. When there was nothing else to do, he would feed firewood to the make-shift hearth to make tea.

Minu never dared to desert them. She would abandon the wish to go anywhere else.

Tima would arrive, followed by Sukadeb. This rehearsal hall was their world. They discussed each other's weal and woe. Minu would smile at times, she would get irritated and angry at others. She would conveniently forget the abuses of elders. Let them say what they wished. If one took to heart all that, one could never make any progress in life. The disturbed Minu would console herself. She would fasten the hem of her saree to her waist and get ready for action.

Minu would take lessons in dance. She would gleefully learn the dance forms of Odishi, Sambalpuri, Dalkhai and Patarasaura. Once into dance, her nimble feet would refuse to rest. While specialists like Gangadhar Sir would crave for rest, she would not. Her *tandav* stance would keep the audience fascinated as though by a spell. When she was merged in a dance, she hardly cared if the ghungroos fell apart or the groundsheet rumpled. Her dance would continue till the song continued and till the music accompanied.

Minu heard the loud shattering of something. She was used to the shattering of glass tumblers or wine bottles but this was different. Despite her unwillingness, she went out and looked around.

Champa was coming upstairs. Sleep hadn't yet unpossessed her. The lines of her *kajal* had become smudgy. Her face appeared blotchy, with the make-up partly washed. The betel juice had made her lips red. She appeared bizarre today.

Withdrawing her look from Champa, Minu asked, "What happened?"

"The chandelier on the ground floor hall fell off," said Champa while climbing up the stairs.

But how could the chandelier fall off? That morning she had visited the hall. Had anyone else gone there after that? How did such a big chandelier fall off on its own?

Minu went downstairs hurriedly. Champa had reported correctly. The rusted chain that held the chandelier had broken. Consequently, the heavy chandelier fell off. The shreds of glass lay scattered.

Minu returned after the inspection. She must send a message to someone to sweep the floor.

How many times she had danced in that hall ! She was compelled to dance for hours surrounded by hungry eyes and thirsty lips. The colourful lights of this chandelier made her wonder at times if it was she who was dancing or someone else. Minu was climbing up the stairs when the Telugu-speaking security guard asked, "Did anything break, sister?"

"The chandelier."

"Chanda…what?"

"Not chanda but chandelier." Minu spoke irritatingly and went inside taking long trides.

Minu's eyelids were drooping with sleep. Usually she loved to sleep in the morning. She went to the bed and lay there. For the last three days, she didn't have enough sleep. She needed three to four hours of sleep for her bodyache to go away.

But who would allow her that much peace and enjoyment! She had just dropped off to sleep when someone knocked at the door.

Pointless anger and helplessness often made Minu burst into tears. She felt like crying today. For the last several days, the memories of the past had been flashing before her eyes, making her feel restless and helpless. She could neither forget the past nor accuse her present. Under such circumstances, she was looking for utter loneliness, which no one could get into. But, who would give her such precious peace in a place like this?

Nabaghan, the effeminate, was knocking at the door. He was a constant source of irritation for Minu. He had neither vanity nor self-respect. He liked his life with feigned anger and deformed ideas.

Minu asked, "What happened?"

"Minu didi, Badadei is looking for you."

"Ok…leave now…I'm coming."

"Please come soon…"

Nabaghana went away. Minu slammed the door with a thud as if to express her anger against him.

She went back to bed and sat on it with her face cupped in her palms. She could no more sleep.

She had spent almost ten years in this trade. Many former faces had disappeared in the meantime. The building had changed its colour many times. The customers had changed their preferences. The girls living in the building had changed their friends too. Minu had heard that some Muslim Nawab had constructed this building to house his concubines. He had also appointed many servants and attendants for them. The mistresses depended on the servants and the property provided by the Nawab. At times, the Nawab would escape from the monotony of his begums and reach here. Those were the occasions when the inmates would burst with joy. Celebrations would ensue.

Minu was reminded of the incidents that had happened to her ten years ago. She remembered how desperately she ran towards the city that night. She felt as if they all ran after her to nab her. If they caught her, they would chop her to pieces. Minu didn't want to die. Despite all the tortures, abuses and humiliating experiences she wanted to live. Two roads lay in front of her. Either she would give up and die or she would run away and struggle to live.

Nobody compelled her to choose the path she had chosen. She resigned to her fate and accepted this place, thinking perhaps this was the dictate of her destiny.

At one go, she had travelled such a long distance. She had successfully evaded death. She wanted to kill herself by jumping into the sea.

She could not die. She was not destined to die that day. How could she die in a day so easily? For the last twenty years, she had been dying every day, every moment. She had suffered untold miseries. How could one, who was destined to die every day, pass away peacefully in an instant?

She was reminded of that dreadful night ten years ago. Unmindful of the thorns and wild growth, she ran under the cover of darkness. The local police found her lying unconscious on the sea beach. They rescued her and brought her to the police station.

Minu could distinctly remember the face of the police inspector. Behind the façade of sweet smiles, he harboured obnoxious thoughts. Minu, on the other hand, appreciated Panu babu. At least, he didn't betray a person's faith.

Oh ! What hungry looks the police inspector had for an hour at her dripping wet and tired body. Intense hunger tortured her body, deep shame tortured her soul. The weak and tired body was inflicted with painful torture. However, her pathetic condition had no impact on that inspector. It generated no compassion in his heart.

He promised to send her to a shelter home but sent her to the brothel instead. That inspector took full share of advantage of her helplessness and till his uniform was totally soaked with disgrace.

Minu had lost her faith in her village, family and in-law's family earlier. She now lost her faith in the police. A married woman with a family was transformed into a whore in the span of a single night.

Many paths lead to the brothel but there is hardly one leading away from it. This is a blind alley. Once you are in it, you lose all possibilities of coming out.

Many thousand times, Minu had hurled the same question at God. How His hands didn't shudder to bestow so much torture, abuse and disgrace on one of His creations?

Idols of stone, clay and paper remained mum. They would lend ear to Minu's complaints. At least Minu would feel as if they lent their ears but they hardly answered back. Minu would break into sobs. No one arrived to wipe those quiet tears. Wiping her own tears, she would return to her room. She would wash away the traces of tears with cold water and soap. She would rub her cheeks and nose with a towel. She would then stand in front of the fan to make it dry. She would apply a coating of powder on it. The stains of tears and traces of fatigue on the face would disappear. Tears aren't adornments of a whore. No one spends money to meet a sobbing-whore. Let her shed tears if she wished; let her have her fill. Let the stream of tears run inside her; let it not stain her cheeks.

At times, Minu would be struck by a sense of wonder. Had she ever dreamt of such a life? All she wished was to have a happy family. A picture of that happy family always flashed in her mind. She wished to have a husband and two loving kids. Her husband would be toiling in the fields. Her family would experience the normal joys and sorrows of life. On the thatched roof of her home, creepers like pumpkin and gourd would run. On the occasion of *Manabasa Gurubara,* she would tattoo the walls with *jhoti* designs. She would draw the feet of goddess Lakshmi, the goddess of wealth, on the ground extending right from the inner rooms to the courtyard.

Most of her dreams remained unrealized. Despite having a home, she didn't have any experience of worldly affairs. Before she could gain experience, she was abused and ill-treated.

Minu arranged her saree and emerged from her room. Badadei had already sent for her twice. She must see her immediately.

Minu's guess was absolutely correct. A new girl had joined the brothel. Her father had married for the second time. The step-mother had two small children. Her father, who was a cobbler, didn't have the slightest hesitation in bartering her for a mere pittance.

Minu was usually put in charges of such new-comers. It was her responsibility to comfort and console them. She could convince others easily with her persuasive skill. She would often say, "In this self-centred world, everybody is governed by his own selfish motives. Who cares for others? You can call two things your own—your stomach and your back. One has to live for the sake of these two. Shedding tears brings no end to the unending days."

Why did Minu fail to convince herself when she could convince scores of others? Why did she crave for a home and a family? Despite having gone through intense suffering herself, why didn't the suffering of another girl move her? What a strange woman she was !

Minu shuddered at such a question. She felt as if someone saw through what she said and what she did. In apprehension, she would lend her ears. She would hear someone's voice, "Minu, you are selfish. You have no home, no husband and no children. You are ill-fated. Therefore, you are envious of the good fortune of others. You can't tolerate if someone else lives a life of joy and celebration. You are a bloody witch.

With her palms pressed against her ears she would shout out, "No...no...no." Her answer reached none. It would dash against the wall in the front and return to her. Tima's wife or Sukadeb's mother might have raised such complaints. It's quite natural for them to put the blame on her for spoiling the son of one and husband of the other. Minu was an ill-fated witch. The good fortune of others made her jealous. She knew some magic and made the young men dance to her tune. She destroyed families."

Such allegations hurt her to the core. Whether the rehearsal was over or not, she would join her palms together and request Tima, "Brother, leave it here and leave for home immediately." She would request Sukadeb, "Please don't stay at the rehearsal hall for such long hours. I find it difficult to put up with so much of accusations."

Tima would console her. He would ask her not to worry so much. He would say that these rustics didn't know the value of song and dance. If one was sinless there was no need of taking the accusations of others to heart. There was no need of banging the head against a wall.

A disheartened Minu would sit, with her head resting on her hands. At one end of the rehearsal hall, Gangadhar Sir would be sitting. He would be sitting stoically, digesting all abuses like lord Neelkantha. He would look at Minu, comfort her and console her. "Don't worry so much. Everything will fall into place. One who charts a new course is bound to have his feet bleeding from thorns. How will life move if one feels dispirited? Had it been so, no one would have dared to chart any new courses. Life would never move if we all took to heart what people flung at us."

Minu would be convinced. She would wipe her tear in the corner of her saree. The play will be staged…no matter what obstacles stand on the way. The troupe would leave for Bhadrak first and then, Balasore. Their troupe would participate in the competition. They would stage new plays. They would procure new clothes and equipment.

Karuni would pour tea from the kettle into each of their cups. Gangadhar Sir would light another country cigarette. The flowing fingers of Sura would glide on the reed of the harmonium. Kirtan would play the kettle drum, producing inspiring sounds. They would all feel lively and energetic suddenly once again.

They would feel as if the rehearsal hall was their real home. They were born for that. The world beyond the hall was a worthless one. The role that people played there was far inferior to the roles that they played. If they didn't play the roles assigned to them in the other world satisfactorily, there was nothing to worry. If they were abused and taken to task, they shouldn't take anything to heart.

Minu lived in such a world. In that world also lived her friends and companions. Oh, what sort of abuses they had to endure !

Minu was somewhat determined to endure all these but it was intolerable on the part of Minu's mother. She found it hard to put up with the condemnation and the vulgar comments of the villagers. When Minu returned home at night, she would find her mother sitting mum, with her gaze fixed at the vast expanse of the sky. The streams of tears would have left their stain on her cheeks. Minu would guess what had transpired. Lying in the bed, she would decide never to go there again.

However, the decision of the night would suddenly change the moment she stepped on the verandah of the rehearsal hall. The decisions arrived at the rehearsal hall would prove futile the moment she reached home.

Minu was listening to the story of the cobbler's daughter from Badadei. After she had finished, Minu asked, "Has her father been paid the amount due to him?"

"Look at her. Listen to what she says. Don't you have faith in me? I handed over three thousand rupees to her father. Umph !"

Not that Minu disbelieved what Badadei had said. She habitually asked that question. She never supported the idea of forcefully picking up someone and inducting her into the trade. She always protested against any such idea. If someone wanted to come on her own, it was fine. Minu would be full of compassion for the one who was freshly inducted. She would feel as if another family was on the verge of degeneration and disintegration. She felt as if another life was going to be sacrificed on the altar of hellish torture. With the passage of time, this compassion would fade away. A strange delight would replace it. Let all families disintegrate. Let all married women turn prostitutes and all married men turn boozers and gamblers. Let the entire world turn to ashes.

Minu would sizzle in anger at the sight of those who reached the brothel on their own or who changed their minds after receiving the advance amount. She had no compassion for them. They were not really chaste but rather excessively pretentious. In a month or two, her guess about them would prove to be true. They should adjust to the aura of the brothel quite well. No matter how obscene it looked, they would lean over the parapet, intentionally exposing the cleavages to attract the customers. They would also invite their attention with erotic talks. They would put on tight georgette blouses with zari border and silk sarees and attract the customers with inviting gestures. They would adorn themselves as dolls and wait on the verandahs.

Minu got up to go after Badadei had spoken. Let the girl stay with them for a week. She would get acclimatized. It was Minu's responsibility to make her feel comfortable.

The girl appeared like a timid bird. She looked all around with wonder. She lacked the courage to say anything or look straight into anyone's eyes.

Her name was Shyamali.

Minu tried to discover herself in Shyamali. There was a time, when she was of her age. Her mother had many dreams about her. Despite the allegations and blame-game of the villagers, she was planning to get her only daughter married to someone.

Minu once again returned to the memories of the rehearsal hall. No one knew what charms that single-roomed house had, which enchanted people like the fragrance of champak flowers. It enchanted all irrespective of whether he played the king or the door-keeper, the beggar or the businessman. Even it took to its lap the small children who collected the imitation swords from the stage. It taught all the art of acting on the stage that included delivering the dialogues with their made-up faces.

Three years passed somehow. They staged their plays at eighteen places during that period. They earned great name and fame for the village. During *Pana Sankranti*, they staged plays in the village for three days. They wouldn't ask others for any monetary help, they banked on whatever they raised from among themselves.

Things took an ugly turn one day. Sukadeb's wife, vexed with her husband, left for her father's home. The in-laws sent messages and sweets to pacify her anger and requested her to return but she refused. One day, Sukadeb himself went to fetch her but had to return, insulted. His wife complained that he was lecherous and immoral. He had illegitimate relationship with Minu. He should better take her as his wife.

Sukadeb returned without success. People came to learn why he had failed. For many days, he was not seen anywhere near the hall.

Minu felt insulted. She shed copious tears blaming her fate. When streams of tear dried up, she burst into a loud laughter. That laughter was much more pathetic than her weeping.

Without marrying anyone, she was accused of

becoming a wife, a concubine. A girl has to live with any one of the two identities. She is either someone's wife or someone else's concubine. She has no other identity.

Minu never thought of harbouring such relationships with anyone. It was not her business to evaluate how others felt about her. She had only one identity—she was Minu, the custodian of the rehearsal hall. She was a friend to all those who were associated with it. It mattered very little how others evaluated her relationship with others.

The rehearsal hall had to accept its share of the blame. It had to withstand many miseries and sorrows. If it could speak, it would have spoken how heavy the weight of the curses were. If it had eyes, it would have shed tears to register its protest.

After what Sukadeb had gone through, the villagers started non-cooperating with all the members of the drama troupe. There might not be anything objectionable in staging plays. But who would tolerate their amorous behavior with unmarried girls? Was there something called piety or not? Heaps of such questions emerged at times from the community mandap.

"Gangadhar Sir would hear about all accusations but remain mum. Some villagers indulge in mean politics. Some affluent persons conspire to forcefully grab the homestead land and utensils of helpless women. Unpalatable extra-marital affairs, forgery and cheating incidents happen at regular intervals. There is hardly anyone who raises a voice of protest on such occasions. When someone usurps the village pasture land, no one protests. When people steal fish from the community pond or when someone decamps with the village deity's ornaments, no one objects. But everybody vehemently criticizes the members of the drama troupe.

Gangadhar Sir would explain, "The taller the tree, the longer its shadow." The more successful one becomes the more censure he invites.

Minu would take into account the arguments of Gangadhar Sir. She would immediately draw plans for the development of the village. Not only song and dance, they had to contribute much more for their village. If the village lost its lustre, what would they be proud of?

All others agreed with her that day.

When all those incidents flashed in Minu's mind today, she thought it would have been better if others had not agreed with her that day. If something was destined to be looted, they should have allowed it to happen. If something was going to be burnt down to ashes, they shouldn't have bothered much. What was the need of protesting so much?

Minu's words were like gunpowder. At the slightest of her indications, people were ready to set fire to everything. These caused great explosions.

The reverberations of the explosion could be heard at the community mandap, echoed at her grandfather's village, reflected at the pond side, felt in the rice fields, and finally landed repeatedly in her mother's ears.

"The drama troupe boys will guard the village pond. They'll take back the community pasture land forcefully occupied by others. They'll go to the police station and register complaints." This was the discussion in the village for some days. People were alarmed. It was as if they were alien dacoits who had come to loot the village and cause terror.

One day Sukadeb's father arrived and told Minu's mother, "Does it augur well that the girl be kept at home without being married off so that she could cause unnecessary trouble to others? Minu's uncle expressed his displeasure saying, "The entire village is defamed for a single girl. I even can't walk the streets with my head held high."

Minu's mother lost the last trace of patience. "Enough is enough. The road to the rehearsal hall will be closed forever for Minu. If she crosses the threshold henceforth, I'll crush the poisonous fruit of the yellow oleander tree and drink the juice."

Minu was prohibited from joining the rehearsal. A fish was deprived of water, a tree was denied of sunshine and a river was forbidden to flow into the ocean.

Frantic searches were made for a match for Minu.

It was as if the entire village could be saved from great calamity if her marriage was solemnized soon.

The village was saved. The fire that Minu had started burnt her to ashes. A widow's family was devastated in that all-consuming fire.

Champa looked very happy. With long strides, she was heading somewhere. Extricating herself from the visions of the past, Minu said, "Where are you going, Champa?"

Champa was looking for someone who she could reveal the joy of her heart. Wiping her lips with the hem of her saree, she said, "Appa, I'm going to see a movie."

"Movie? With whom?"

Champa didn't say anything. She only flashed a smile.

Minu didn't ask anything more. A young man visited Champa frequently. He spent hours in her company. At times, he abused her in a loud voice. He was a rich man's son. He loved her.

Did anyone love a whore? Minu found such a proposition unacceptable. Might be true, who knew? The young man told her stories and sang songs. He bought her a variety of gifts. Champa loved him in return.

Minu considered that the heart of a woman was very strange. One could win it either for a few boxes of cosmetics or for a few metres of ribbon. Even a saree was enough.

Champa was in a hurry. Minu said, "Go…Champa… go. You might be getting late." Champa flashed back a smile with happiness. Her happiness did spread a feeling of joy in and around the place like wavelets created in a pond.

The brothel was a strange world. Variety of men came

here. It was very hard to keep a tab on them all. Minu didn't display any fancy for one until he approached her and talked to her. But many types of news reached her. When things got out of control, she volunteered to negotiate peace.

A few days back a strange incident happened. A tall and dusky man came to Laxmi's room and started beating her. Laxmi didn't know him earlier. Why should a person, hitherto unknown and unseen, arrive one day and beat someone? Later she came to learn that he was a businessman. During his stay in Laxmi's room, he continued beating her. Before leaving, he threw a bundle of notes onto the floor.

Had Laxmi wished, she could have got the person arrested. Didn't a whore feel pain? Didn't she feel hurt when one beat or chopped her to pieces? Strangely, Laxmi didn't seek anyone's help, not even Nabaghan's. She kept lying on the floor, hours after the man had left the place.

Minu came to learn about the incident the next day. Despite the best of her efforts, she couldn't know the real reason. She had met a great variety of characters in her life. Some men seemed more pathetic than helpless women. They failed to express what ailed them. They burnt themselves flamelessly and their life got reduced to ashes in the smoldering fire.

That man didn't visit Laxmi after that incident. Laxmi should have felt happy and relaxed. Strangely, she wasn't happy. How much she wished the man should come !

Why did Laxmi wait for that tall and dusky businessman to arrive? Did she wish to disrobe him and watch his nude body? Did she wish to peep into his heart and discover reasons of his suffering? Minu never understood. She only understood that the man bore some pain, some inexplicable sadness and suffered wordlessly.

Minu understood another of the secrets. A woman would often become eager to understand the man who wriggled out of her clutches. She always wished to bring into her control something that lay beyond her reach. She aspired to attain something that was difficult to attain.

The shades of sorrows are different. Minu was reminded of the sorrows of her mother. She visualized her face in death. It looked grey like a half-cooked brinjal. Her husband had passed away much before his parents did. She had hoped that she would get her daughter married off before her death and die peacefully. But, that simply couldn't happen.

Many proposals came but they failed to materialize. Wearing clean presentable clothes, applying make-up on her face, carrying tea and snacks on trays, Minu would appear before the members of the groom's family. However, things wouldn't proceed much. All these seemed like rehearsals to Minu.

She heard that many scandalous tales concerning her were doing rounds in the market place and on the pond side. That information must have reached the elderly relatives of the prospective grooms. This brought a premature end to all the proposals. Why should a gentleman have a tainted girl as daughter-in-law? When these tales reached Minu, she would block her ears with her hands. What sin had she really committed? What was her fault?

After the death of her mother, Minu felt entirely responsible for her death. She hardly knew what was father's love and affection. Before she could realize the warmth of that relationship, her father had said good bye to the world, to shine as a star in the sky. Her relationship with her mother was deep. She grew up basking in her love, affection and blessings till she was twenty four. What could she give her mother in return, except tears, grief and sighs? The funeral pyre burnt in the cremation ground. The fire and smoke soon disappeared. Her mother's ashes were washed away by the rain. Her physical body merged back in the five elements of nature. Except memories of her mother, nothing remained.

Minu wiped away her tears. Where from tear drops appeared after such a long time !

She was orphaned after her mother's death. A young woman of twenty-four turned an orphan. The world to her looked dark and frightening. The protective roof from over her head collapsed.

At this juncture, Minu's uncle came forward. He took upon himself the responsibility of her marriage. It's true that her father was dead but her uncle was still alive. The villagers heaped praises on him.

Within days of assuming the responsibility, Minu's uncle was able to fix her marriage. Something that her mother had failed to do in three long years could be done in three months.

The prospective groom was the owner of abundant landed property. The only problem was he was a little aged. Did it really matter? Age isn't an important consideration in case of a groom. Not many problems related to dowry cropped up during the negotiations. Still, something had to be given. "You all know about my poor financial condition." Minu's uncle would narrate in greater length about the troubles he faced in life.

Minu understood quite well why her uncle suddenly started taking great interest in her. Despite knowing it all, she would remain mum. Who would listen to her even if she spoke out the truth? The villagers had already excommunicated the members of the drama troupe. Sukadeb's father led the group of such people. Who would she tell her worries? Who would she request to collect some information about her prospective groom and his family?

Minu remembered quite well what happened one day after her mother's death. She was feeding the burning hearth. Her uncle and aunt came and sat by her. Her uncle sat on the cot. Her aunt sat by her near the chullah and broke a cow dung cake into two, to feed the fire in the hearth.

Minu was in discomfort to see her uncle and aunt together. She was reminded of her mother. The tears flowing from her eyes evaporated in the heat of the fire. Whenever Minu felt angry with her uncle, her mother would pacify her, "One's uncle is like one's father. He always thinks of the welfare of his niece. You shouldn't talk evil of him. I know he was not in good terms with your father but he never ill-treated you."

Her aunt broke the silence to say, "Listen Minu, this is not good. Perhaps no villager talks on your face, but they put the blame squarely on us. You are alone. You can share what we cook. What's the need of cooking separately?"

Minu couldn't hold back her convulsive sobs any longer. She burst into a loud wailing.

Minu's mother had told her that her uncle had made fun of her father before separating from him. "He is an actor, an effeminate human being. He is worth nothing. I slog in the fields and get wrinkles while he enjoys himself acting in plays." Till his last days, father never forgot the denunciation and abuse by his brother. Despite grandmother's wailings and advice of neighbours, uncle was bent upon separation. Why was he insisting on patching up things that he had torn apart years ago?

Minu said, "Why do you worry, aunt? There are as

many hearths as there are families. Why should someone unnecessarily blame you?"

Aunt bit her tongue. Addressing her husband, she said, "Do you listen to what Minu says? She says there are as many hearths as there are families. It's true. There are as many families as there are male members. You are like an outsider. Till the moment you get married, you belong to this family. After marriage, you will belong to another family. You start your own family thereafter. You are just a temporary guest here. Why should you have another hearth?"

Aunt wasn't wrong. The life of a girl is like that. The family into which she's born and the house that reverberates with her childish prattles don't belong to her forever. The family about which she knows nothing and its members, whom she has never met during the first twenty years of her life, become her own. She has to live the rest of her life with them.

Her uncle had assumed the role of a guardian. "No way...she can't have a hearth of her own. She'll stay with us. She'll eat here...sleep there." Otherwise, he would go on fast indefinitely.

Minu was compelled to soften her stand. She remembered what her mother had told her once, "Uncle is no less than one's father. Man's words can spread poison or nectar. No doubt, her uncle had spoken many offending things in the past. But, it was the same uncle who had come to her with offers of renewed relationship. How could she say no? Minu cowered her head and said, "Aunt, have you taken all decisions?"

Aunt didn't have any answer. She looked in the direction of uncle and said, "Are you listening? Why don't you tell something about the groom's family from Kalapata to Minu?"

Her uncle cleared his throat and said, "Had there been problems, I would have certainly brought to her notice. Why should I trouble her for nothing? The family has no dearth of houses, landed property or cattle. Minu is extremely lucky that she is getting married into such a family. If we miss the opportunity, we are surely going to repent later." Then looking at aunt he said, "You know, sister-in-law had tried her best to get a suitable candidate for Minu but she failed. Getting a suitable groom is not an easy job. Besides, the play rehearsals in which she participated…" Uncle deliberately kept rest of the information unrevealed. The benefits of holding back such information are many. No one could find fault with the person who spoke not. On the other hand, the listener understands everything implicitly. Each unspoken word hits her causing immense pain.

Minu wished to revolt. What harm was there if she was associated with the rehearsal hall? She was proud of it. She had done something that others in her village could not do. What was there to be ashamed of?

She could not express her feelings. She had no courage. Her backbone had broken completely. She had received a terrible setback after the Sukadeb incident.

She heard them in silence. Minu's aunt held her hand and took her to her house. Aunt sprinkled water on the fire in the hearth to put it out. The entire room was filled with smoke. The smoke brought about tears to eyes. That day, Minu shifted to uncle's house.

She left her father's place, re-establishing her trust in the quick-sand of relationship. She didn't return there anymore. She herself made way for her uncle to take over the property. Her uncle soon took possession of the room--the room in which she was born, the room in which her mother had anointed her tender body with a mixture of oil and turmeric paste. Like Duryodhan establishing control over Hastina without even spending a pie, Minu's uncle cunningly took possession of her paternal property without investing a pie.

The villagers, on the other hand, went on heaping praises on her uncle. They argued in no uncertain terms that it was a herculean task to arrange a groom for his characterless niece like Minu. Minu stood alone along with her so-called stained history on one side and on the other stood her uncle, aunt and the villagers. Her marriage was arranged. To defray the expenses, her paternal homestead land and other landed property were mortgaged.

Minu knew that her uncle was milking benefits from all the property that her family had once possessed. The talks about village money-lender, debt and mortgage were nothing but means cleverly conceived to usurp property that they owned. Minu knew it quite well that her marriage had, in no way, left her uncle in debt, he was rather benefitted immensely. In fact, he was doubly benefitted. He received a sum from the groom's side for arranging the marriage and secondly he got rid of her and became the sole owner of all the property.

Whenever this thought crossed Minu's mind, her body ached and heart bled, as if she was walking barefoot on thorny bushes. The hooded serpent of greed that lurked behind the veil of good relationship would appear demoniac to her.

She came across those feelings much later—after she had started setting up a family at Kalapat.

Her marriage was going to be solemnized. Minu had participated in marriages, several hundred times on the stage. But this time, the very mention of the word marriage made her bashful. How would the groom look?

Who else would be there at his home? What would be their expectations from her?

Minu had no one to bring her such vital information. Tima had been absconding. Sura had left for his village. Karuni no more came to her in dread of the villagers' bashing. Kirtan had become a bonded labourer. Who would she ask for information? How could she ask Gangadhar Sir all such questions?

But, why Tima went missing, without informing anyone? Minu would often feel that he was somewhat mysterious. He could not say what he wanted. He would often talk about things that he had no business of talking about.

The marriage was solemnized—marriage of an orphan. There was more of compassion than happiness, more sympathy than affection. Gangadhar Sir arrived and was found standing by the palanquin meant for carrying Minu. He raised both his hands to bless her, "Go…Minu… go. Accept everybody as your own with affection. Set up your own family. Let happiness kiss your feet." Minu's sobs, hitherto withheld, broke loose as she leaned herself on to his solacing shoulders for emotional strength.

There was a murmur of discomfort among the crowd. Minu had touched the untouchable. She had despoiled all her piety and purity.

Minu found it difficult to restrain herself when her palanquin crossed the rehearsal hall. She thought she would jump off the palanquin, run to the hall, shut herself inside and go nowhere. She would rather spend the rest of her life here.

The hall was lying deserted. Only Karuni stood near the disfigured signboard. There was no one else in the vicinity. Her much revered rehearsal hall looked dilapidated, much like a podium deserted after marriage rituals. Minu burst into tears. The inside of her chest writhed in pain. All memories and dreams associated with this hall floated in her thought in an instant. For the last seven years, this hall was her home. Her relationship with it was going to be severed forever.

Through a chink in the curtain, Minu looked at the hall. She found Karuni shedding tears. Minu's heart softened for Karuni. He was standing like a defeated lone soldier, next to a fort that had been ravaged. Two streams of tear had run down his cheeks before drying up. The only consolation was that at least there was someone in the world who cried for her ! Nothing more could be expected for an ill-fated orphan.

The palanquin crossed the village. A deep convulsion emerged from Minu's inner core chilling all her bones within. Her relationship with the village, its boundary, its fields, its pond, and its *Kendu* grove were snapped forever. Who knew whether she would get another opportunity to be with them.

In fact, she never met them again. She never came back to the village--the village where she had taken birth or the village soil on which she had played her childhood games. Everybody deserted her. Everybody forgot that Minu had existed once upon a time. She had no father, no mother and therefore, someone should have looked after her. But no one did. No one came to apply soothing balm on her raw wounds.

Minu's palm reached to caress her left thigh. She felt as if the burn-wound hadn't healed till today. It looked reddish like the petals of a hibiscus flower.

No... the wound had healed...years ago. However, the wound that the incident had caused in her heart would never heal. It would torture her soul till death came to take her back.

Minu looked through the window. A jeep screeched to a halt nearby. It soon departed, after someone had got off. Minu turned her face inside.

This brothel was the hunting ground for everyone. The unemployed youth, local goondas, politicians, police officials reached here any time they wished. The Police could reach here anytime—even at odd hours. The officials would knock on the door. They would pick up sleepy-eyed people, put them in the van and take them to the police station. The person would have to spend the night in the company of mosquitoes and fleas. The farce would go on throughout the night for a fine of five hundred rupees or at best a thousand.

Why is a woman's life like this? She is hardly allowed any peace of mind; she is hardly allowed a space of her own. Doesn't she have the right to her personal joys and jubilations? The questions would go unanswered. She would concentrate on other tasks at hand. These days, she escaped easily from police actions. Earlier, she had to endure much. She had already mastered the art of taming the tiger and making the deer dance to her tune.

That was a different story altogether.

Minu fixed her gaze on the walls. The colour on the walls had peeled off at places, giving it a weird look. The curtains had become dirty. She replaced the bed-sheet and the pillow covers and put the old ones on the ground. Nabaghan was expected to take them for a wash.

The curtain-less doors and windows made the room appear lacklustre like a widow's home and much like the life of Minu.

Minu got married and like other brides, she went to her in-laws' home. When the nuptial knot was tied on the marriage pandal, she felt delighted at the touch of the rough hands of a man. During the *kaudi khela* the touch of the hand on her palm and fingers filled her with a strange delight. For a moment she thought she had landed on a solid world. There was no question of slipping off or falling down. The land beneath her feet was firm and stable.

With the hope of a firm and stable world, she waited for her husband in a dark room of the house with a low thatched roof. She had dreamt of forgetting sadness forever and bearing welcome smiles on her lips. In the flickering light of the gloomy lamp, she had drawn the portrait of a glorious future.

However, Minu hardly got an opportunity to dream. She didn't even get the opportunity to smile. She was born to cry, how could she smile?

The man that she discovered in the faint light was a dark-complexioned, obese and dwarfish elderly person. He might be a few years younger than Gangadhar Sir. He sat on the edge of the bed and gazed at Minu silently, like an invalid hyena greedily watching a rabbit trapped among the creepers.

Minu burst out a loud yell. The moist wick of the lamp, the thatched roof and the closed window panes shook. She got up from the bed and jumped to the ground, as if she suddenly discovered a snake hiding below the cushion of her bed or pillows.

Minu's husband was startled. He shuddered in fear. Was Minu mad? Why did she give out a cry like this? After roaming around the room for some time, he opened the door and ran away.

Minu stood leaning against the wall of the room for a long time. Drops of perspiration appeared on her forehead. An uncomfortable agitation churned inside her. Her hands and feet shuddered, like plantain leaves in stormy rains. Had she stood there some more time, she might have collapsed to the floor. A wide bed lay in the front. A white sheet lay on the bed. Minu didn't feel like going to the bed. She felt as if the snake lay hidden somewhere there. She spread the hem of her *saree* and lay on the ground.

She could not know when she fell asleep. She had many dreams. She saw the trees laden with *gulmohar* flowers. The sky was suddenly overcast with dark clouds. The red *gulmohar* surrounded by dark clouds looked extremely enchanting. She ran through a foot-path in the jungle. The cold turbulent wind was leaving her heir dishevelled. After running over a long distance, she came to a dense tree and sat in its shade for rest. Streams of sweat ran all over her body. Her chest heaved. A corner of her saree was lying on the ground. She was taken aback when her eyes suddenly fell on the saree. The red saree that she had been wearing had suddenly turned white. Her hands looked bare, there was no colour anywhere. Confused, she gazed at the sky. All the *gulmohar* flowers had fallen from the branches. The surrounding appeared deserted. The bare ground burnt in the midday sun.

Minu's sleep was disturbed. She felt like crying loudly. She was reminded of her mother and her endearing words. She frequently remembered the dreams that her mother had about her future. However, she couldn't cry loudly. She knew her crying would have no meaning as she was in an alien village, surrounded by unfamiliar people. Can someone be pampered by people who were in no way related to her?

She consoled herself. She wiped her tears with her palm. She felt she had to live with whatever she had got. This was going to be her life.

It's since then that Minu cultivated the habit of putting up with all the troubles without raising much of a clamour. No matter what happened with her, she never made others have an inkling of that. What was the use of disclosing the secrets to strangers? They would display eagerness to know more and feign compassion but only derive malicious pleasure.

Once, the thought of returning to her parents' village had crossed her mind. But who would be there? Who could she call her own? She was an unfortunate bird. After having deserted her nest, she discovered that not only the nest was damaged but also the tree that held the nest was uprooted. Her mother passed away a few months ago. Her father had passed away before her. Without parents, their house meant nothing but despair. Where would she go now?

Minu often wondered why fate was so cruel to her. Was this the fate of a princess that the astrologer had talked about? Was this called good luck?

Perhaps the astrologer of her childhood days knew the truth but didn't disclose it. Perhaps he didn't wish to incur others' wrath. Why should someone try to invite someone else's ire unnecessarily? Here, every one eagerly wished to be endeared by others.

Minu didn't wish to invite the ire of others too. She wished to endear the members of the in-laws' family, the cattle, dogs, trees, creepers, and all others. Even that aged, obese, dark-complexioned man was there in her list. But she couldn't succeed.

On being reminded of the experiences of those days, she would shudder in fear. She would visualize a red hot iron spatula. Its broad surface appeared red hot, like the tongue of a wild dog at night. She would shut her eyes in fear. Her sister-in-laws, although she had none her own, would often say that she was fortunate to have been blessed with immeasurable wealth besides a small family to take care of. She should rather live like a queen.

Minu would listen to their talk. At times, she would add a sentence or two. She would smile at times but did never reveal the secrets. She would finish taking bath quickly in the village pond and return home. She would light the hearth and bow down before the sacred Tulsi. After she had drunk the water into which her mother-in-law had dipped her toes, she would eat *pakhala* with smashed brinjal and dried up mango. Her entire day was spent in peeling off of vegetables, grinding of spices, washing clothes, readying the utensils for lunch and dinner besides cooking and eating. Minu had no leisure even to gaze at the sky. But she was satisfied. How would she spend her leisure? Whose thoughts would she be lost in? The thoughts that she was concerned with only made her cry. They would have forced tears from deep inside her eyes.

Minu would somehow spend the day. However, she would find the night time difficult to spend. Even the brief nights of summer seemed endless to her. She would hanker for someone's warm intimacy. She would wish to put her head on someone's chest and convert her tears into laughter. She would wish to gaze at the stars in the sky and dream. But her wishes were never fulfilled. No one knew where that scorpion was; it appeared at the right time and hid itself under the bed. Her husband, after a brief intimate encounter, would fall asleep and snore. Driven by the repulsive sounds of snoring, sleeps refused to come to her eyes.

This was how the nights were spent—nights with an aged and impotent individual. The first half of the night was spent in wait and the second half in neglect and regret.

Gradually, everything was laid bare before her. She realized well that she had been cheated. Her uncle and aunt, in order to grab the homestead land, the field where vegetables were grown and four *gunths* of land of her father's share, had got her married to an aged and impotent individual. They had traded her for fulfillment of their selfish desire.

Minu wished to invite all the scorpions and snakes living nearby and allow them to walk on her. She would lie on the ground nude and the scorpions and snakes would move everywhere on her. Her body would turn blue with their poison. She would die—die for thousands of years and never be reborn. No matter how much one tried, the poison should never go and she should never come back to life again.

She would wait eagerly for some magic to happen in the middle of the night. She would feel thirsty again and again. She would get up and drink water from the pot without making others realize that she was awake. The touch of the cold breeze would set her body on fire. She would look at the bed, to find her husband lying inert like a wood-idol. His deep snoring made his chest heave. Otherwise, it was difficult to know if he was alive.

Her nights were spent in constant waiting. On some occasions, she would never get a wink of sleep throughout the night. She would get up with a sigh. Day would dawn. From the tamarind tree, which had its branches spread all over their house, the crow would caw. A sense of desperation would grip her.

This apart, there were the household chores like cooking, slicing of vegetables, grinding of spices, massaging of mother-in-law, serving husband and sitting near the threshold of the kitchen. In the afternoon, she did exactly what she had done in the forenoon. It was nothing but a monotonous repetition.

Did all these mean 'household chores'? Was it what in-laws' house meant?

Minu couldn't accept all these. It was against her nature to accept anything without logic. It was not her nature to follow trodden paths.

That was the full moon night. A bright moon lighted the whole sky. Minu took a bath and put on a new saree. She put to use all the experience of 'make up' that she had acquired from the rehearsal days and adorned herself. She felt confident.

That night, she didn't allow her husband to sleep early. She didn't even feign to have fallen asleep, suppressing her injured feelings.

After the day's hard work, Damodar had been tired. The sight of his wife in new clothes surprised him. Was she his wife or a fairy? He had never ever seen such a beautiful woman in the entire village.

On many occasions, sensuous feelings would take shape in him. But they utterly failed to materialize due to some undetected deficiency. Every time that deficiency was shattering his manliness into dust.

Finally, he closed his eyes in sleep. But, Minu didn't wish to sleep so early. For her, there was still much time left in the night. Her hopes and desires remained to be fulfilled.

She climbed on to the bed. She raised the wick of the lamp. The room got lighted. She took off all her clothes and sat on the tummy of the dark-complexioned and obese husband. She rubbed her husband's nose with her own. She tickled him at his waist. She turned and twisted around his chest. She had a thirst that was seven fathoms deep. Her throat felt parched. Her bosom, arms and the space between her thighs created a sensation. She wished that Damodar should get up. He should fondle her body and quench her thirst. He should hold her in his lap and lull her to sleep. The rest of the night should be spent in amorous talks. She moved from Damodar's waist towards his chest.

Damodar got up and gave out a loud yell before jumping from the bed. In confusion, Minu was thrown off. While she was whispering 'What happened, what happened,' he unbolted the door and escaped to the courtyard. She tried to decipher what exactly had gone wrong. She was angry with herself for causing unnecessary trouble. In shame and anger, she quickly gathered her scattered apparel and covered her nude hunger.

She had never imagined that the moment she opened her eyes in the morning, she would be confronted by an unpleasant scandal.

The entire village believed that Minu was a spirit. She ate her victims raw. The previous night, she had climbed on to her husband's chest and was about to use her teeth to draw blood from his neck. Damodar was fortunate that he got up in time. Otherwise, he would never have seen the morning sun. He was fortunate to have survived.

Minu was branded as an evil spirit.

She ate her victims raw.

She stealthily went to the cremation ground during dark nights. Before leaving home, she would charm her husband to deep sleep by chanting incantations. That sleep was not so easy to break. On return,she would take bath and chant another incantation for her husband to wake up. Death was certain for anyone who came face to face with her while she was on her way to the cremation ground. At the sight of that apparition, even a butcher would collapse.

Since that morning, people became uncomfortably aware of Minu's changed incarnation. Her routine life underwent a transformation. Words spread that at night she changed into the form of a strange spirit—a spirit who swallowed her victims raw.

Damodar was also transformed into an incredible creature at the end of the village and in the paddy fields. He had returned with life from an encounter with a female fiend. He himself had witnessed the nude incarnation of the spirit. He had also witnessed how she burnt brightly and how her tongue looked blood red. Damodar didn't hesitate to feed the curiosity of the interviewers in great detail. People stood stunned and listened to his accounts in juicy details.

"There must be a mole in the middle of the bosom. There must be a black mark just above her heel. If these two signs are there, be sure she is a devil. She is supposed to swallow the victims raw." The experienced villagers would advise Damodar convincingly.

"You must feign sleep. Sing the name of lord

Ram while sleeping. The antics of the fiend will become ineffective if you chant the name. When your wife leaves for the cremation ground throwing away all her clothes, just go after her, collect the clothes and burn them. The female fiend will no more be able to return to you," someone else advised.

Damodar would return home and inform his mother what the villagers had said. He would obey the advice in letter and spirit. He would pull Minu by her hand from the kitchen and drag her to their bedroom. There he would ask her, "Take off your saree and your blouse, quick."

Minu would feel bashful. On the other hand, Damodar would be burning in anger and disdain. His nostrils would be flaring up. Minu would take off her saree and blouse. Damodar would search for something from her nude body and shout, "You are a devil. There's no doubt about it. See, there's a mole here." He would suddenly fling open the door and run away to tell others the secret of the black mole on the forbidden part of her body and disclose the unknowable secrets spots of his wife's breasts and thighs to the public.

He wouldn't even wait till she wrapped herself in her saree. He would hear no explanations from her. What a pity ! This man was supposed to be the master of her present and future life. Pressing the hem of her saree on her eyes, Minu would burst into tears. Warm tears would run and moisten its folds.

Suddenly, everything in Minu's life went topsy-turvy. Her mother-in-law didn't accuse her of anything directly, but she didn't allow her to come close to her anymore. She was no more dipping her toes in the bowl and leaving the water for her to drink. In fact, Minu didn't like to drink the water in which someone had dipped her feet. So, she didn't at all feel disheartened by the decision that her mother-in-law had taken. Only her efforts to remain away from her made her feel disoriented.

Damodar did no more share the bed with his wife at night. He was certain that his wife was a female fiend. He was fortunate to have got up in the middle of the sleep. Otherwise, he wouldn't have witnessed the sunrise the following morning. He would examine his feet and palm carefully three or four times a day. He had heard that the spirit drew blood through the wound on the feet or the palm. He would feel restless even if he found an ant-bite mark on his body.

Minu was left with no option other than blaming her fate. Throughout the day she would keep herself busy in the household chores. She would wash clothes of the entire family, clean the mats and ground sheets, draw water from the well and water the plants, sweep the verandah and the courtyard two times a day. She wanted that she should grow tired and her limbs should grow inert by the end of the day. Consequently, she would fall asleep the moment she went to bed. It was difficult to remain wide awake in anticipation of things that simply refused to happen. Impeded by sorrows and suffering her time lacked the enthusiasm to pass quickly.

Despite being worn out physically, Minu could never sleep in peace. A stream of events, though faint, would float before her eyes. Minu would see her own figure in that. She would feel as if she had gone to bed without changing into fresh clothes. She would get up and change clothes in the dark. Worried that the clanging of her bangle would disturb the sleep of others, she would untie the knot of her saree quietly. She would relapse into the bed after changing into fresh clothes.

That night she didn't even close her eyes for an instant.

Damodar was already asleep and snoring profusely, as if he hadn't slept for nights. Sleep eluded Minu's eyes. The acid smell of Damodar's sweat and his raucous snoring prevented sleep from descending upon her eyes.

Minu slept facing upwards. Her hands lay crossed on her bosom. The two palms rested on the two breasts. The breasts hadn't lost their firmness. A deep sigh emerged from inside, quaking the chest bones. She hid her face in her palms and burst out into unending sobs.

How strange the hunger of the body is ! No amount of food or drinks can subside that hunger. Minu opened the door and came out to the courtyard. She then opened the door towards the well and went out. A line of banana trees stood on both sides. Through the leaves of the coconut tree that stood adjacent to the boundary wall, the faint moon was seen hanging from the sky. A combination of light and darkness had spread everywhere. The banana leaves shook in the wind. Minu closed the door from outside, lest Damodar or her mother-in-law should get up.

There was much greenery in the backyard, under the open sky. Under the influence of the faint moon, Minu wished to forget the distressing experiences of hers. There was a panoply of stars strewn all around in the sky. Minu proceeded towards the coconut tree. A black cat suddenly crossed her path. Minu was startled. With her back resting on the stem of the coconut tree, she stood for some time.

She felt stifled inside. The four eyes of Damodar and her mother-in-law, like four thousand eyes, followed her wherever she went. When she took bath near the well, her mother-in-law would arrive there in pretext of collecting spinach. Collecting these was an excuse. Her intention was to keep an eye on Minu. In the process, she deprived her even a moment of privacy.

That night, Minu was all alone. Damodar wasn't expected to get up before morning. Minu removed the saree from her shoulder. She unbuttoned her blouse and removed her bra and hung them on the tree trunk. She looked at herself. She could perceive the craving of her limbs for love. She outstretched both her hands to embrace the night breeze and the moon beams. How tranquil the touch of the cold breeze was ! How intimate the silence of the shadowy night was !

Minu wanted to embrace the bent coconut tree with both her hands and sleep on it. A gust of breeze blew away her white saree from the trunk towards the banana trees. Minu ran to collect her saree.

In the meantime, the black cat mewed loudly as a mouse or some other prey escaped from its clutches.

Her mother-in-law's sleep had broken listening to the sound of the back door being opened. She got up on hearing the cat. The door at the back stood open. Some distance away, among the banana trees, there stood a tall woman, with her hair left loose. She gave out a loud howl and woke her son up, "Dama…Dama."

By that time, Minu had put on her saree. She had never expected that the sleep of the mother-son duo would break at this odd hour. She shouted and said, "Mother…it's me…I have come to the backyard."

Minu rushed in, reached her bed and lay down on it. That night, she could sleep tight. The exhilarating experience of the cold breeze on her bare body filled her with pleasure.

Damodar and his mother couldn't sleep anymore that night. They stood, gazing in bewilderment at each other for a long time. They harboured no doubt that she was an evil spirit who swallowed her prey alive. Every night, she would escape to the fields on the backyard through the back door, but to-night she was caught red handed.

Damodar was busy throughout that day in connection with the sale of an ox. He didn't wish to sell a strong and stout ox for a paltry sum of seven hundred rupees. He had even decided to take the animal to the cattle market, if he didn't get the right price for it. But, the absurdities of his wife made him forget everything related to the sale. He gave the least importance to all his work and ran to the exorcist, Parameswar, for a cure.

How many rumours were rife in Kalapata centering Minu ! She sucked the blood of children in an instant. She did go to the cremation ground and feasted on excreta and piss, while moving around upside down. She sat on branches of trees with her legs held apart and sucked the blood of all passersby. Parameswar, the healer had thrown some sparks from his country cigarettes on Minu's saree to confirm if she was enchanted. The next morning Damodar himself ran up to his village to pass the message that the sparks on his wife's saree had created holes in it.

Parameswar, the healer would visit them. He would caress his bald head and look around. His gaunt chest would swell up in pride and arrogance at the thought that he was the savior of the entire Kalapata village. Had he not protected the village, the anger of ghosts and demons would have burnt it into ashes.

Minu's husband and mother-in-law took shelter under Parameswar, the healer. After the scandal broke out, they found it difficult to walk through the village. Little children and young women of the village stopped going by their home. The villagers had almost ostracized them. Under the circumstances, only he could provide them respite.

Parameswar prepared a list of all the items required for the ritual. It included brooms, a bucket, a new grinding stone, tail of a stingray, an iron griddle, and nails.

Minu was left to rot without food and water in a closed room. A twenty-five year old orphan was left to suffer untold miseries and abuse. She was left alone to shed tears. She would condemn her fate. At the same time, she would feel astounded to note how she had put up with so much sorrow and abuse.

The sun rays played on the verandah like a carefree girl child. A great deal of noise emanated from the village streets as a lot of activities went on. A few were returning from the village pond collecting water, whereas some others were returning from the village temple. Someone was returning from the village fields where as someone else was heading towards the market. Children would soon return from their schools. The cattle would return after grazing. The noise would reach its peak before subsiding. The din of cattle, sheep, goats, hens, ducks, cats, dogs, pigeons, mynas, and cranes would take some time before settling down. The tinkling of the cycle bells, the screeching of the bullock cart wheels and the clinking of the bells around the neck of bulls would gradually dissipate. Everything in this world would begin to expand, decay and dissolute. There are ups and downs in life as in sounds. Confined to her room, Minu would witness the game of beginning and the end, she would hear all sounds appear and disappear. In the tiny pond of her mind, a pebble would create ripples before disappearing from sight. With the passage of time, she would find a sky full of stars. Like the sky of the dark fortnight, her future appeared doomed. Her unfulfilled desires gazed at her expectantly like the innumerable stars blinking in the sky. While shoving firewood into the burning hearth, she would lose her concentration. The froth would enter the hearth. The fire would extinguish, filling the entire place with smoke. Minu's absentmindedness would terminate.

None of the neighbours came to chat with her. If someone had some work with her mother-in-law, she would return from the front verandah after meeting her. If Minu came in view, mothers would cover their children with hem of their sarees and depart soon. No one wished to meet with her.

On the other hand, unspoken thoughts would be restless in her mind to get expressed. She wanted to share about her days in the maternal uncle's house, including her climbing on the trees and swimming in the village pond. The memories of the rehearsal hall didn't allow her any peace of mind. Who would she lay bare her heart to?

The discomforts of the night were more torturous than that of the day. Each moment of deceit and abuse passed like an aeon. Damodar would sleep on another bed and snore. He didn't have any appetite for love; he didn't have the desire to fight. He only knew how to slog like an ox, swallow food and sleep. Minu would always wish to release herself from the fetters that constricted her, open the door and escape. That seemed a better option than enduring the persistent abuse.

However, she could never gather the courage to escape. Her mother-in-law and suspicious husband monitored her movements. Besides, there were the hostile neighbours and the anxious villagers. The sound of a cumin seed bursting in hot oil was exaggerated as a cracker. Minu's behavior and manners were a hot topic for gossip among the villagers.

Parameswar, the healer came to drive away the spirit. His forehead was smeared with red vermillion. He looked very much like a painted jackal. When Minu was reminded of the proceedings of that day, her hands and feet would shiver in dread and she would drench in sweat. She would desperately search for an escape route like a mouse that desperately tried to escape from the cat on one hand and the landlord on the other.

The smell of resin and incense spread everywhere. Red cloth, red hibiscus and vermillion were collected along with new brooms, tail of a stingray, a grinding stone and a pestle stone. Minu took bath, put on new clothes and sat on a low wooden stool. Drops of water trickled from her loosened hair. The atmosphere inside that smoke-filled room suffocated her. Minu gathered courage and sat on the allotted seat with downcast eyes, just like a culprit before village panchayat.

After chanting some mantras, Parameswar asked, "Who are you?"

The children, women, old men and old women, and men who gathered around her house lent their curious ears to hear the answer.

Minu couldn't understand the intention behind the question. She answered in a whisper, "Minu."

"False ! Absolutely false ! You evil spirit ! You fiend ! I won't admit to any deception. I'm a specialist—a *solakalasadhaka* complete exorcist. I have exorcised many *Brahmarakhshas* and ogres in my life. I've confined many devils to the banyan tree at the cremation ground by nailing them there. Do you think I'm a fool to accept your treachery? Tell me the truth. Tell me who you are. Otherwise, I'll whip you with this tail of the stingray," Parameswar yelled.

Minu grew dreadful at the thought of whip from the tail of the stingray. The dry, thorny tail lay on a low wooden stool. It looked like a sword. The flesh had disappeared, only the bones and thorns remained. She spoke in a whisper, "I'm telling the truth."

"Lie of the basest kind ! The exorcist yelled again. He picked up a china-rose and touched Minu's forehead with it. Next, he picked up the thorny broom and smacked seven blows, carefully counting seven times. Minu wasn't prepared for this sort of ill-treatment. Blood oozed from several places on her fair body. Her back and arms ached. She wailed out painfully, "O my mother ! Save me ! I'll die if you beat me like this. Please don't beat me."

Parameswar, the exorcist gave out a loud guffaw. A shiver ran through the smoke-filled room. "She'll certainly leave this place. No doubt about that !" He said this and started chanting incantations once again.

Minu sat there with downcast eyes. The blows with the thorny broom caused immense pain not only on her body but also in her heart. She gazed with disdain at Damodar, the person whose hand she had held in marriage for her protection.

For the residents of Kalapata, this was only but an opportunity for rare recreation. They all watched the farce and derived pleasure. They all waited with bated breath for the moment when the evil spirit would shun the body of the daughter-in-law of Nayak family and disappear into thin air.

Parameswar, the exorcist repeated the question. Minu was afraid of getting another round of blows. She didn't know what to say, or what to do. She only sat with a bent head and downcast eyes. She held her teeth tight. Let him beat her, whack her, chop her to pieces…let him do what he wants to do. She craved for life no more; she begged to live no more. The sooner the soul deserts her body the better.

The exorcist grew tired soon. Smoke had got into his nostrils, making him cough. He was losing his hold on the situation. This was enraging him. He got up shouting *kling*,

kling and landed a few more lashes on Minu with the tail of the stingray. The tail made a swish-swash sound while it cut through the air. Then it would land on Minu's back, head, thighs and shoulders. Minu lay on the ground writhing in pain. She was heard saying, "Please don't beat me…please don't beat me…please leave me alone…I'll leave this place and go away. Please allow me to go."

Damodar was stunned by the entire episode. The small children scurried back to their homes. The young ladies concealed their faces under extended veils.

A stream of sweat flowed down from Parameswar's emaciated body. The entire forehead looked red with the vermillion smeared everywhere. He looked like a blood-thirsty jackal. He stopped whacking Minu and said, "Go… go away. Leave this place this instant."

Minu arranged her saree and started running. She could only cover the distance up to the coconut tree and fell unconscious.

Nabaghana appeared and said, "Didi, the police inspector was looking for you yesterday."

Minu stopped doing her hair and said, "Why didn't you inform me?"

"I came to inform you. You were mumbling something in sleep. I called many times but you did not respond. The inspector said, "Let her sleep. Don't disturb her. I'll come again in the evening."

"What business did he have?"

"I don't know. I think you know better…"

Nabaghana implicitly indicated something. He always talked like that. Earlier, Minu would feel vexed. These days, she didn't lose her temper anymore.

"Ok…Ok… go now."

Nabaghana went away. After seeing him depart, Minu shut the door. If Panubabu had come, why did he go away without meeting her?

Different types of people visited the brothel. Some of them reached surreptitiously, some others arrived in disguise in broad daylight. Some of them bargained for flesh where as some others negotiated for the heart. Minu would feel like laughing. Which man had wealth enough to purchase the heart of a woman? Some of them would try with sweet nothing talks like "I love you." But they are afraid to say this in broad day light. Their hands and feet would shiver. They would carefully look in all directions to be sure that they are unnoticed.

Some people arrived under the cover of darkness, donning fine silk Punjabis and draped in silk shawls. They would smear themselves with perfume and carry garland of jasmine. Such people would condemn the brothel in broad daylight. They would accuse it of being the breeding ground of syphilis, gonorrhea and many other dreadful diseases. They would file petitions requesting the municipality to throw away the premises out of the town. They would clamour for the prostitutes to be sheltered in destitute homes. The moment evening descended, their puritanical mind set would disappear into thin air. Morning targeted assurances of the evening; evening failed to espouse the promises of the morning.

Minu never considered the brothel as a place of pilgrimage. She didn't consider it a holy place even the day she was compelled by circumstances to enter into flesh trade. Nor did she consider it as a holy place now. However, she found it difficult to accept that the place was 'no better than hell'. Hells existed everywhere. Why should the brothel or the prostitute be singled out for censure?

That day, her body, mind and soul were on fire. She was burning like the flames in the ignited hearth. The combustion was sufficient to burn her into ashes. She had made an attempt to save herself from the funeral pyre. Before she realized where she was heading, what she was doing, whether she was doing everything right or anything wrong, she had become a prostitute. Despite being a prostitute, Minu had never repented. Even the prostitute enjoyed some freedom. The daughter-in-law of Nayak family of Kalapata didn't have any of that.

Parameswar, the exorcist sprinkled some cold water

on Minu lying unconscious near the coconut tree. The moment she opened her eyes, she found the torturous healer in front of her eyes. She grew so scared that not a single word emerged from her mouth. Her eyes had turned wide. She experienced pain all over her body. She had marks left from beatings all over her limbs. She experienced a burning sensation. It was as if someone had rubbed salt on her wounds. She simply joined her palms and said, "Please don't beat me. I am not a fiend. I am Minu. You may kill me if you like but please don't beat me."

Many times, Minu thought of taking poison. She would take the name of God and fall asleep forever. But how difficult it was to arrange poison ! Even, she thought of tying a sand filled pot around her neck and drowning herself in the pond. The thought of hanging herself from the wooden beams of the roof of her in-laws' house also was an alternative option. But she couldn't do anything of that sort. Even at the most sorrowful moments, someone enticed her with the thought of remaining alive. That invisible spirit told her that her sorrowful days would surely end. Why should she commit a sin for future births by committing suicide?

Finally, Parameswar the healer announced that Minu was possessed by the spirit of Damodar's first wife. The entire problem stemmed out of the jealousy of the co-wife. The spirit would never leave until the entire household was completely destroyed.

Damodar wasn't concerned about the ill-fate of his wife. He was sad that she had arrived to cause immense damage to his household. Perhaps he thought if somebody else had been there in place of Minu, the spirit of the former wife wouldn't have possessed her. The fault lay with Minu and Minu alone.

Minu felt startled at such a revelation. Her uncle and aunt had kept it hidden from her that Damodar had already married once before. She felt terribly angry with them. However, they lived too far away. It was improbable that the news of her miserable fate would reach them.

When Damodar was twenty eight years of age, he had brought Savitri of Patapur as his bride. She had lived with him for four years. But, one morning her dead body was found floating in the pond of the monastery.

"But why?" Minu asked this question to many. Some of them would avoid the question altogether, some others would leave the place after heaping abuses on her. Savitri was six months pregnant when she died. How could Damodar's wife become pregnant? The question itself answered Minu's doubts. Her pregnancy was illegitimate. No doubt, she died fearing social stigma.

Savitri had grown scared. After her wishes were fulfilled she committed suicide. Wasn't death a favoured option than living life as Damodar's wife?

The insatiate soul of the promiscuous Savitri was supposed to have been roaming around Kalapata village. It was roaming around Damodar's house, backyard and barn. Since Minu had taken up her place, her spirit took possession of Minu. The anger of a co-wife was more spiteful. Her spirit would either taste victory or be vanquished completely. She would never leave it unfinished.

Minu found it difficult to understand how such stories were concocted in the matter of a night and spread so quickly among the villagers. She would also find it difficult to extricate herself from the scandalous misinformation campaign that enveloped her like a cobweb. Her objections, complaints, earnest requests, anger, tears and sobs were meaningless. She would look on helplessly.

At times, she would think of fleeing to her father's place. At least Gangadhar Sir would understand her feelings. He knew her quite well since her childhood. Would he ever believe that Minu was a spirit or an immoral girl?

However, she would find it difficult to go there. Books, newspapers and speeches of great people would appear meaningless to her. The fate of a woman is suppressed under a huge boulder; she is like a doormat, and she is like a dustbin where people leave the dirty stuff before entering the platform.

How long had she spent at her in-laws' place? Only five years. However, the five years looked like five ages. Each year looked like one aeon. Lack of affection, deliberate neglect, doubt and exploitation made her emaciated. She was losing her interest in food and clothes, sleep and drinks. Wherever she went, ignominy followed her like a mad dog.

She was a fiend.

She was a promiscuous beast.

She was barren.

A huge mountain of grief would crumble on Minu, burying her. The false and baseless accusations of being barren would make her breathless. She understood why Savitri preferred to die by drowning.

Had she not died by drowning, they would have killed her by inflicting torture on her every moment.

One day, she decided to face her mother-in-law boldly. It was the month of harvest. Her mother-in-law had just returned after winnowing paddy in the barn. Minu had just returned after lighting the lamp at the sacred *Tulsi* plant. Clearing her throat she said, "Mother, why are you heaping all the blame on me?"

"Who should be blamed then?" Her mother-in-law said feeling utterly vexed.

"I won't say. How can I say whose fault it is?" Minu didn't wish to put the blame on anyone in particular.

That day, her mother-in-law misunderstood her. How dare you accuse others by saying, "I won't say…I won't say"? It's a habit with you to talk haughtily. You have disreputed both your father's family and your in-laws' family with your immoral activities. Aren't you still satisfied?"

Minu felt immensely hurt. She ran back to her room. She entered inside and closed it. She sobbed bitterly till her anger and injured feelings flowed like water of the stream.

Who would she speak to what she felt inside? Who would she say, "Just look at me. I am fertile. I have wishes and desires. I also yearn to hold a baby in my lap. I yearn to hear my child calling me, 'mother'. I never wish to die childless and barren. I wish to be a mother."

Someone made fun of her. It was her fate.

Minu spent days without taking food or drinks, trying to reconcile with her cursed fate. She condemned herself for being the wife of an incapable man. She was compelled to live with the infamy of being a fiend and a barren woman.

Damodar would never sit silently. He would conveniently put the blame on his wife. How ill-fated he was ! He was married twice but on both the occasions, he became the lord of two barren women. Two barren, infertile pieces of land !

The villagers, who regularly received a supply of betel cones and *biri*, expressed their compassion for him. They consoled him, "Wait for few days more. If there's no news, you can get married to a *sahada* tree and bring home another wife."

"If you wish to have a child, there's no harm in marrying any number of times". The village pundit would consult the scriptures and quote appropriate lines. Damodar would feel relaxed and assured. Minu's mother-in-law would pour a generous portion of rice and some money into the pundit's bag. The pundit would tuck his palm-leaf scriptures under his arms and leave the place happily.

Minu wanted to curse such a flattering Brahmin. How dare he pave the way for another girl to come to spoil her life ! Another ill-fated girl would be tied to the altar of sacrifice. Why should she be the wife of an impotent fellow but be dishonoured throughout her life?

But there was still some time for all this to happen. Minu still lived as the daughter-in-law of the Nayak family.

On the recommendation of Parameswar, a *batiskala* exorcist was invited from a far-away city. It was planned like this. On the no moon night, he would arrive from the cremation ground while continuing to chant incantations, exorcise the evil spirit, take it away with it to the cremation ground, and nail it on some tree. His incantations were undoubtedly effective. Irrespective of where the evil spirit hid, there was no escape for it.

Minu had to encounter that ill-fated night once again. The darkness of that night was deeper and more ferocious.

The new exorcist looked like a rhinoceros. In the labyrinth of his moustache and beard, his lips and eyes almost disappeared. He had wrapped himself with a black shawl. He had beads of rosary, some round and flat talismans, four garlands of bones and shells around his neck. Marks of vermillion on his neck and forehead burnt bright red. Together with the bloodshot eyes, his appearance was so terrifying that none other than elderly people dared go near him.

Minu appeared in new clothes after having taken a bath. The village was deserted. Kalapata village lay in deep sleep. Through the coconut leaves nothing other than a panoply of stars was visible. The exorcist, having come from the funeral ground, sat on his seat.

Minu grew afraid the moment her eyes fell on the exorcist. The tail of a stingray lay within his reach just as Parameswar had one a few days back. An iron spatula, thrust into burning wood charcoal, appeared red hot.

Minu lost her consciousness.

Her emaciated body, bewildered mind and betrayed soul couldn't tolerate the sight. She didn't know how many more times she had to encounter this living death.

That exorcist sprinkled some water on her face to get her back to sense. He read out the *mantras* quite loudly now. He asked her curious husband and mother-in-law to go out of the room and then asked her, "Tell me who you are."

Minu remained mum. The exorcist picked up the tail of the stingray with his right hand and smacked her once. Minu felt as if her flesh and bones would fall apart. She pressed her teeth tightly to endure the pain. She had already realized that she might have to undergo torture as many times as she presented her true identity. There was no respite for her. Besides, the entire world had already declared her a fiend. Parameswar had already proved that she had been possessed by Savitri's spirit. No matter how much she tried, she could never release herself from the identities thrust on her. Whether she accepted it or not, she was a fiend. She was not Minu but Savitri. The exorcist examined her once again, "Who are you?"

"Sa-vi-tri."

The exorcist was taken by surprise. He appeared perked up. He called out to Damodar and his mother, "Come and see the efficiency of a *batiskala* exorcist."

Minu started play-acting. Acting in the rehearsal hall

had once led to the door of hell, now with the help of acting she wished to get respite from there. She closed her eyes that day and prayed for only one thing, "O God ! Please grant me respite from here. Please !"

Since he hadn't received any answers even after putting the question twice, the exorcist picked up the tail of the stingray. A startled Minu said, "I'll go away from here. Please leave me alone."

"You bloody evil spirit ! You won't leave this place so easily. For the last five years, you have been causing trouble for everybody." Then the exorcist called out to Damodar and said, "Come here. Hold both of her hands. Just hold them tight."

Damodar rushed in readily. He held both the hands of Minu tightly with his own hands.

Minu gave out a loud cry. She thumped her legs. She used all the energy that she could muster to escape. Her attempts proved inadequate. The heartless exorcist picked up the red hot spatula, lifted her saree and pressed it on her thigh. The red hot spatula scalded her flesh. She screamed with all her might. "O God ! O God ! Please save me. Here I die !"

That horrendous cry pierced through the silence of the midnight village. The owls resting on the tamarind tree flew away, causing a flutter. A terrified Damodar dropped Minu's hand and got up.

The exorcist shouted, "Go away and leave this place for ever."

Minu got up. She didn't look at anyone even for once. She didn't wipe her tears. She started running, dragging her left leg that caused immense pain. She ran straight, without turning in any direction, no one knew where.

That obese, rhinoceros-looking exorcist ran after her

with the hot spatula in his hand. Minu had run too far ahead of him. She had left Kalapata village, its narrow lanes and the red gravel roads too far behind. In the deep darkness of the night, even her own shadow was difficult to trace.

The scar left by that hot spatula existed on Minu's left thigh even today. The three inch wide scar just above the knee would continue to exist till she lived and would accompany her to the grave.

Minu often found it difficult to fathom how she was able to run such a long distance. Only one thing was certain that she was running for life. If she escaped from them, perhaps she would be able to survive. She would survive to die a death of her own choice. Otherwise, they would chop her to pieces and burn her alive.

The day had already dawned. Minu took a look at her dress. Despite being surrounded by so much sorrow, she felt like smiling--a wry smile. She mocked at her body, her youth, her mind and her soul. Even a beggar woman would appear healthier and more attractive.

Lack of sleep, weariness, hunger, thirst, and the wound on the thigh made her distressed. That moment Minu made up her mind to jump into the sea and give up her life. She had no mother, she had no father, she had no home, she had no husband and she had nothing to boast of. What else was there in life to remain alive?

However, Minu couldn't die. She was thrown back onto the beach, half-dead. Her fate had guided her here.

Scarlet red resembling the colour of blood was smeared on the sky even though evening had already descended. The darkness of the night, despite its best efforts, couldn't erase the redness. At the sight of it, one grew dreadful, fearing that some calamity might strike. There might be a thundershower or a storm.

Minu was collecting stars in the palm of her mind from the sky-garden. When she was a child her mother had told her, "It's inauspicious to gaze at a lonely star." When she saw a small star next to the evening star, she felt reassured as though she got respite from a big calamity !

At times, she liked to gaze at the sky. The patches of cloud changing their shape and size delighted her. She associated her fate with the fate of the stars and struck a conversation with them. Until her wearied eyelids drooped with sleep, she would lean on the window, look at the sea and gaze at the sky.

However, she didn't have any control over nights. On certain nights, she would not see the sea, not even once. Her body would grow so tired and mind so indifferent that she would wrap herself in a blanket and fall asleep. By the time she left bed in the morning, it would be quite late. Then, it wouldn't be possible to gaze at the sky.

Nabaghana appeared and said, "Panu babu is waiting

for you in the office. He has some urgent business with you."

Minu switched off the fan, closed the door and went to the office.

She had developed acquaintance with Panu babu for the last four years. He worked as an inspector in the Town Police Station. No one else had worked there for such a long time. He was an extremely hard working person.

She had met Panu babu by chance. Minu had shut her eyelids. She was ready for the moment when an unknown hand would denude her and play with her nude body, the way a hunter played with a tiger he had shot dead.

Surprisingly, Panu babu didn't demand anything of that sort that day. At the sight of Minu, a different feeling had cropped up in him. But why? Hadn't he met another prostitute like her in the forty-two years of his life?

Minu said, "Why are you lingering? You must be getting delayed. Come and let's get it over."

Inspector Pranakrushna shuddered a little. Did any prostitute invite a customer like this? There was nothing vulgar and lustful in that invitation. It was a kind of indirect threat…an order in the guise of a request…straightforward talk.

Pranakrushna said, "Come and sit by me. I'm in no hurry. Let's talk to each other for some time."

Minu wasn't delighted. She had neither patience nor time for prolonged conversation. The sooner her job was over, the better. She would then go to her bed and take rest undisturbed, or she would cry freely without any inhibition.

Pranakrushna was not in a mood to leave the place early. Minu got up and switched on the light. Bright light illuminated the room. In that light she saw that he was a strong and healthy person. His hair had been cropped close to the scalp. He sported moustache that resembled the whiskers of a tiger. A few hairs on the moustache and the beard had turned grey. He had put on a neatly ironed out white shirt and trousers. He smoked one cigarette after another.

Minu had encountered different types of people in the brothel. Taking their character and behavior into consideration, she named them after animals and birds. Someone was named buffalo; someone else was named pig, while others bore the name dog or crow. Such naming helped her to examine the person besides filling her with childish delight. The vulgar and uncomfortable moments passed in such pastimes. She would lie on the bed like a rubber doll. Her body was no way connected to her mind; her mind was no way connected to her soul.

At times, she would grow ashamed of her life. She would think of getting up in the middle of one night so that no one could spot her. She wished to run far away somewhere. But, her past would hound her memory. She would visualize a person running after her with a burning hot spatula. If somehow he caught hold of her, he would press it everywhere on her. He would etch on her that she was a fiend and an immoral woman.

The brimming tear would roll down. Where would she go? In the entire world, there was not even a little space for a woman. She didn't have the right or freedom to live alone. She could neither go back to her in-laws nor was there anything called father's family. She knew quite well that no one would accept her. No one would grant pardon to a woman who had deserted her husband and run away. If she wished to live, it could only have been with her in-laws, at Kalapata village. For that she had to put up with the infamy of being a fiend and a woman of disgrace, the tortures of exorcists, and the tortures inflicted by her husband and mother-in-law without protest. She had already lost that opportunity. She could never go there. The door to her in-laws' house was closed forever.

How enchanting a picture of the in-laws' house her mother had portrayed ! When Minu was a child, her mother would put her in her lap while feeding her and talk about her future. Minu's father would find a prince-like husband for her. A blessed Minu would manage her worldly affairs for hundred years. During festivities, he would give them an abundant supply of gifts—sixteen loads to be precise.

Minu had added her own dreams to the paradise portrayed by her mother. She had gathered some information from the experiences of sisters-in-law and aunts in the neighbourhood and painted her own world. She had learnt the tricks as to how to grow acquaintance with a bunch of hitherto complete strangers and how to grow intimacy with them. She had heard that when she entered her in-laws' house after marriage, she had to boil some milk and let it overflow, wishing wealth, children and all round prosperity. She mentally prepared herself to live such a life.

However, not a single dream was fulfilled. Not a single portrayal of imagination matched with reality. Rather, dreadful accidents that she had never ever dreamt of and never ever dreaded happened, shattering her dreams forever. Finally, she was to become a prostitute.

Pranakrushna spoke about him for long. She enquired Minu about her family and home. Minu wanted to erase the memory of those from her mind. She wished never to remind herself of the unpleasant past. She didn't want anyone's compassion either. She was like a student who learnt her lessons every morning on a clean slate. Like him, she also started her life afresh every day. She had no past, no future to boast about. She had hardly any relationship with her past.

"You look like the daughter of a good family," said the inspector.

Minu didn't say anything in reply. Such remarks weren't usually responded to. She was disgusted with him. Was she his beloved? Was she supposed to gossip with him for hours?

Her anger subsided after listening to what Pranakrushna had to say. After that, she wished to love the man. She even repented of having lost her cool.

The inspector's wife had left her seven years ago. She didn't wish to become a mother. She wished to enjoy the pleasures that absolute freedom and abundant wealth could bring. Pranakrushna's police job with his extra income even couldn't suffice her demands.

How insatiable a woman's desires and infinite her demands could be !

Minu was very happy to hear the accounts of the inspector up to this. Let all households be devastated. Let all wives abandon their husbands. Let all husbands beat their wives mercilessly and drive them to the verge of death. Let all households be reduced to ashes by the fire of disenchantment.

Minu was terribly angry with the rest of the world. Here there was no place for kindness, compassion, love and affection. Only selfishness, jealousy and suspicion ruled the roost. Why should she be bothered whether such a world existed or turned to dust?

Pranakrushna, under the veil of the police man's dress, was a strange person. He had been yearning for his wife even now. He still had hopes that his wife would return. Waiting for her, he spent his otherwise married life alone.

Pranakrushna's words made Minu's heart heavy. How much her life was different from that of the life of this man ! Things would have been different if Damodar had loved her one-hundredth times this man loved his wife. Had it been the case, why she would have fled from her in-laws like an orphan in the middle of the night !

The feeling of helplessness is more corroding than being really helpless. She had none to call her own; there was no one to give shelter even for a moment. This helplessness made Minu feel decimated.

In the alien world, she had grown some acquaintance with Pranakrushna that day. She hoped perhaps he would be able to render some help at the time of need.

Pranakrushna appeared in police uniform. Minu was surprised to see him like that. Why did he choose to arrive at this hour of the evening, that too in uniform? What was the purpose? What did he have to do with her? He could have reached Minu's room without anyone's permission.

The moment Pranakrushna's eyes fell on Minu, he got up from the chair. He walked slowly towards the door.

Minu shrank within the moment she saw him. A very strange fellow this man was ! He never allowed anyone to take advantage of his acquaintance with him. When he appeared in the police uniform, he forgot to be kind. He refused to do any favour. At times, he appeared terribly insistent.

She was reminded of the first time they both had met. After a prolonged discussion, when Pranakrushna left the room, he offered her a few crumpled notes.

Minu, with her hands at her back, answered

courageously, "Without consummation, I don't accept compensation."

Pranakrushna grew a little surprised. Minu paid him no heed. She stood with her hands at her back.

"You have done your duty. This is the fee you deserve…" Minu looked solemn. She said, "How helpless you want to make a prostitute! First, whatever you demand has to be fulfilled by her. Then, you force her to do something that she doesn't like to do. Do you know how helpless one becomes when she receives a fee just out of compassion? Had you realized this, you would never have tried to insult me."

The currency notes in Pranakrushna's hand returned to his pocket. He climbed down the stairs and went away without any reaction.

Had Minu not encountered him that day, she would never have understood how cruel and ruthless a person, who had given in to her harsh words during their first meeting, could be.

Many days back ! Badadei had forcefully picked up a girl through the pimp and tried to induct her into her group. The matter somehow reached the ears of Pranakrushna. He reached alone at the brothel and conducted a raid. How vicious and untamable he looked then !

Badadei requested him to take a seat. Minu knew that she had offered him an amount of fifty thousand that day. Pranakrushna shoved the bundle of notes with his baton as if it were a cowdung-cake. He arrested Badadei, rescued the girl and took both to the police station.

No one in the brothel could spend those three days peacefully. Finally, a worried Badadei told Minu, "Please do something to get me out of this place. Otherwise, this haughty officer will send me to jail."

To Pranakrushna's ill luck, the girl's father changed his statement when he was paid the fifty thousand rupees that Pranakrushna had vehemently refused to accept. Pranakrushna's demeanor was worth seeing that day. Like a wounded tiger, he was ready to pounce on everybody. At the sight of the girl's father, he was rushing towards him threateningly.

Pranakrushna ! He appeared calm although there was a restless sea roaring within. Usually, he was quiet but within minutes he would lose his cool and get ready to burn down everything like fire. He would hold a person by his collar, pick him up and drop him down on the ground. Or he would beat him mercilessly without caring how much pain he caused.

Pranakrushna's appearance at the brothel was as welcome as it was a cause for concern. Who knew on what pretext he would lose his cool and cause trouble? His two eyes weren't mere objects to see things through; they were like the headlights of a jeep. Not even an indistinct thing like a needle could escape his investigative eyes.

Minu knew that Pranakrushna appreciated her and had a soft corner for her. His feelings for her weren't the feelings that usually existed between a prostitute and a customer. But she never tried to take advantage of that feeling. She never demanded a closer intimacy with him.

Why had he arrived in police dress at that hour of the evening? Had it not been something serious, he could have summoned her to the police station.

In an alarmed voice she enquired, "What's the matter?"

Pranakrushna asked, "Do you know Champa?"

"Champa?"

"Yes, Champa."

Minu wasn't mentally prepared for this kind of police examination. His eyes, lips and manner of talking seemed so vastly different and unacquainted. In a diffident voice she said, "Yes, I know her."

Pranakrushna appeared unruffled. "She passed away last night. Her dead body is lying in the City Hospital. You have to go there and identify her. Come fast."

Minu had never thought that she would come to get such a piece of news. She thought might be, the villagers of Kalapata had reported to the police about her missing. Police might have come to the brothel looking for her. She heaved a deep sigh. For a moment, she felt reassured. The next moment, she turned sorrowful. How come no one cared to find out where she suddenly disappeared and whether she was alive or dead ! How worthless her life was !

The news of Champa's death made her more sorrowful than her own grief. Even though they lived under the same roof, the news of her unnatural death hadn't reached her. The moment she got this news, Champa's smiling face flashed before her.

For the last few months, a particular young man had been visiting her regularly. Champa must have fallen in love with him. The young man took her to the theater. They spent the evenings on the beach. She adored the young man. Honestly, Minu hadn't bothered to keep more information about the duo.

Pranakrushna said, "Get ready and come quickly. It's an urgent case. Let me go now."

While going to the City Hospital in a rickshaw, Minu was thinking about what Pranakrushna had told her. It was no less a consolation for her that the death of a prostitute was being considered an urgent case. Only death can bring glory to those who live a sinful, exploited and debauched life.

She got off the rickshaw and went to the casualty outdoor. Inspector Pranakrushna was waiting for her.

The Inspector said, "She was pregnant. She was carrying a six-month old foetus. Perhaps she had gone for an abortion and died there. They dumped her body by the side of the hospital boundary wall. She had tattooed her name 'Champa' on her hand. Besides..." Pranakrushna whispered to avoid the presence of the driver... "I had seen her a couple of times in the nearby areas. So, I could recognize her easily."

"Then..." Minu asked.

"Someone else should identify her." Then...

"Then what?"

"The dead body will be handed over to her relatives."

"Relatives? Which relative will come forward to claim the dead body of a whore?" Minu's voice reflected her disappointment.

"Otherwise, the unclaimed body will be sent to the mortuary."

Minu fell silent for a moment. She was astounded by the cruel truth indicated at by Pranakrushna's statement. Mortuary ! She had heard that the unclaimed bodies were stolen from the medical campus. "They are transported to different places and dipped into acid barrels. Acid melts the flesh, skin, hair, and fat. The bones and skull are transported to the traders." Perhaps Champa's body was going to meet the same fate.

A smiling face continuously flashed before Minu's eyes. Champa had arrived at the brothel three years back. Her father had sold her to the pimp for the sake of money and wine. The flesh of young ladies is in great demand in the flesh market. Perhaps no one would visit them to accept them as daughters, daughters-in-law or as sisters. However, there would be a beeline of people ready to display their virility on nude women throughout the night in exchange for some money.

Champa arrived as a fresh commodity. For many days, she didn't talk much with others. She would remain mum most of the time. Perhaps, she couldn't accept this unusual life.

Even during those days, Minu had been entrusted with that despicable responsibility. She was asked to induct her to the business of prostitution.

Minu grew terribly angry with herself. She felt ashamed and grief-stricken. Her jealousy and intolerance had made her do what she had done that day. She wished that everybody should turn a prostitute; everybody should be deserted and exploited like her. If she was found unworthy of a blissful life, why should anyone else spend her time in bliss?

How could she turn so selfish? How could she become so cruel? Minu felt as if there was no trace of compassion left in her. During the last ten years, everything noble in her had burnt to ashes. Just as iron rusts on exposure to sea breeze, all her emotions, sensitivity, delicate emotions had rusted. Has she not compelled Champa to accept prostitution, she mightn't have met this fate. She mightn't have died too.

Had Champa really turned a prostitute? Never ever had Minu seen greed for money in her eyes. She always wished to love someone—someone with who she could smile, play and share her feelings in the moonlit night, in the lonely park. She was always in look out for such a person. She never offered herself at the feet of someone in lure for a bundle of money.

Minu realized that Champa had been betrayed. Her young heart, which craved for pure love, had been deceived. On the pretext of loving her that young man had dragged her to the doorstep of death. Either he had feigned that he would marry her, or excessive faith in that young man made her embrace motherhood. The yearning to set up a family and become a mother perhaps forced her to pay with life.

Mother !

In the prostitute lanes, who is worthy of being called a mother or a daughter?

Here motherhood was a figment of imagination, a thing borne in the mind only. To carry it really in the womb was forbidden. The one who dared to wear the shackle and enchain herself was surely going to repent later.

Despite all these prohibitions, didn't the desire to become a mother make her restive? Didn't it make her heart and soul crave with desire? Hadn't the enchanting desire of holding a baby in the lap and remaining awake night after night made her impatient?

Yes, it had. That enchanting desire made her restless many times. It made her go crazy at times. Whether on the street or in the field or at the market, at the sight of a child stuck to its mother's laps Minu's heart would cry out in distress. The exasperation of her sighs often made her mind heavy.

On many an occasion, she had strangulated her motherhood. She destroyed those seeds of creation in her womb many times by swallowing obnoxious pills and some loathsome potion. She could neither muster courage nor had the ability to bring them to the world. There was no use indulging in those thoughts anymore. Today, even the incessant rains of the *Shravan* wouldn't be able to germinate a blade of grass the dry desert of her life, leave alone the possibility of bearing a flower.

Minu had deliberately converted herself into a barren land since the day she had given in to prostitution to make a living. She had taken such a decision in her rational mind. Now, she was only a prostitute, a play-thing of flesh and blood. She was no more a mother or a woman with the possibility of motherhood.

Why had Champa gone to commit such a sin? Under what temptations? Under what delusions? Had she given birth to a son or a daughter, would her fate have changed? Would her abused adolescence and battered youth have returned? No, nothing of this sort would have happened. Nothing would have changed. Things would have gone the way they were going. She would have lived with another disgrace till death. The innocent child would have borne the disgrace without any of its fault. It would have lived with the identity of a bastard. Would he or she have been grateful to its mother for bearing him?

The child would have reproached its creation. The society would have reproached the creation. All would have joined hands together to reprove her and call her a 'prostitute... and nothing else.'

They were prostitutes. It's true that they weren't born as prostitutes but they would surely die as prostitutes. No one would shed tears for them. No one would accompany their bier or participate in the obsequies rituals. The wood on their pyre would be arranged by the grave digger employed by the authorities at the cremation ground. Their body would burn into ashes; their identity would vanish into nothingness.

It's true that some people visited them quite regularly and promised to build castles for them while some others praised their song and dance. But none of them was expected to be there by their funeral pyre. They visited the flesh market, paid for the commodities just as they would pay for the fruits and vegetables they bought. They sucked the juice and went away discarding the squeezed fruit, leaving it to rot in the sewers of the society.

Likewise, Champa's dead body would rot in the mortuary. It would be boiled in the acid pot and the remnants would be sold in the market. Her body was sold when she was alive, her bones would be sold after her death.

Champa's insatiate soul would roam around in the world. Nobody would offer her even a drop of water.

Minu's eyes were searching for someone. If she could meet that boy, she would pull him by his hair and rain blows on him. To hell with his love ! To hell with his virility ! If she met him, she would take revenge for killing a helpless girl in the name of love.

Champa's body was lying on the stretcher. Her tummy and bosom had at first been cut open and stitched later as if she were not a human being but a sack of rice.

Minu cried bitterly.

The tears overflowing from her eyes weren't ready to accept any impediments.

How helplessly Champa's dead body was lying in a deserted condition ! This was the dead body of that girl whose smile could cheer up the surroundings. When she talked, the heart of the most sorrowful person enlivened. She now was there in front of her like a lump of flesh. Minu covered her face with her palms and retreated a few steps. She covered Champa's face with the white shawl that the police man had taken off while showing the body to her.

Pranakrushna asked, "Has anybody arrived to claim the unclaimed body?"

The hospital sweeper and the constable gazed in the direction of the OPD counter. Diverting his attention from there, Pranakrushna told Minu, "You can go now."

Minu wiped the tears with the hem of her saree and said, "I'm one of Champa's relatives. I'll take her dead body. Please help me a little."

Pranakrushna was surprised. Minu had to pay a price for being emotional. She would not only have to spend some money but also be subjected to much disgrace. This was a police case. She would have to run to the police station and attend to court frequently if she were associated with an unnatural-death case. Besides, where would she carry the dead body in the darkness of the night?

Minu was bent upon taking the body with her.

"She was my younger sister. When no one else has arrived to claim her body, I must carry it with me. I'll arrange her funeral. Otherwise, her soul won't attain salvation."

Pranakrushna fixed his gaze upon her. Minu appeared more mysterious to him. Every time he met her, he discovered something new in her personality. Was she only a whore?

Minu got into the van with the dead body. She gave necessary tips to the sweepers and the attendants. Irrespective of what happened to the patient, they would never help unless they were paid handsomely.

Pranakrushna wanted to stay with Minu to help her. But, society would never accept him rubbing shoulders with a whore. He summoned the constable, ordered him to help Minu, got into his office vehicle and returned.

Minu looked around as if searching for someone. She wished to request someone to summon Nabaghana. Who would she request? Wasn't it a sin to ask someone to visit the brothel? No one dared to look, during daytime, at the faded two-storeyed building that stood beyond the drain, near heaps of garbage. Who would she send there during so late in the evening?

Minu looked at the police constable. Even though he appeared in police uniform, he had adorned himself with sandalwood paste on his neck, forehead and arms. On his neck, he wore three layers of *tulsi* beads. At least, he couldn't be asked to go to the brothel.

How would she do everything herself? She felt helpless within. She fished out a twenty rupee note from her purse and handing it to the constable said, "Will you please pass the message on to Nabaghana? I want him to come."

The constable thrust the note into his pocket and said, "This is the case of my boss. I am not supposed to accept a single pie. Please wait here. Let me go and find him out."

The constable took his cycle and disappeared soon.

It was eight in the evening. The cremation ground on the sea beach was deserted. The police van left Champa's body on the sand. The white shawl covering the dead body began fluttering in the wind. Any moment, it might fly away. Champa's fair-face shone like the moon but she didn't get up and sit.

The sea breeze was making Meenu restless. From the centre of the cremation ground, ash emanated from the smouldering fire and flew in the air. The pots, bier and the mat that had been carried along with the body were lying on the spot. The relatives were visible nowhere.

Minu's acquaintance with death was quite frequent.

When she was a child, she lost her father. After she grew up, she lost her mother. Even though she was grief-stricken on those occasions, she wasn't needed to see the desertion associated with the cremation ground. Champa's death had turned her death-minded. She felt as if something within her was dying an unnatural death. She felt as if her own, and not Champa's body, was lying on the sea beach.

How helpless man is ! How hollow man's vanity and pride are ! She wished she should embrace death that moment. She had lived enough. She had neither a present nor a future to boast of. The city was hardly concerned whether she was alive or dead. Nothing would come to a halt when she died just as nothing had come to a halt with Champa's death.

A bicycle was seen coming towards her. It must be Nabaghan.

It was midnight by the time the obsequies were over. Standing by the side of the pyre, Minu felt singed. Besides, she had to take bath at an odd hour. The alternate heat and cold wore her out. The portion below the knee refused to budge.

Nabaghana also had become tired. Minu was very compassionate to him. Everybody made fun of him by calling him an effeminate person. He would gel well neither with the females nor with the males. He was neglected by both. His life hung in the middle. Just as a whore is never respected among women, similarly Nabaghana was never respected among men. When there was some task to be done, everybody sought his help. They would tip him with a ten rupee note to get their work done.

Nabhaghana spent his time in the brothel, bearing all the discomfort of a worthless life. He himself was in no way responsible for the weakness for which he digested all insults. He wore strange clothes; his manners were bizarre. His manner of talking and ways of walking were grossly unconventional.

Minu never made fun of Nabaghana. How could she, who herself was an object of ridicule, ridicule another person?

While returning from the cremation ground, both Minu and Nabaghana expected that the brothel would have become deserted, grieving the untimely demise of Champa. Since the news of her death was handed over by a police official, everybody in the neighbourhood must have come to know about it. Since the day Champa's drunkard father handed her over to the pimp, this brothel had become her world. This was the place where she danced, sang, smiled and shed tears. She was earning money for her sustenance and for the upkeep of the brothel.

As they approached the brothel, Minu's hopes dissolved into thin air. Contrary to her expectations, the brothel that day wasn't deserted. No one was found shedding tears, nor was anyone found consoling anyone grieving. The place was busy and crowded as it usually was on other nights. There were few rickshaws parked near the entrance. People were found loitering around the wine shop as usual. Nothing seemed to be missing.

Minu felt crestfallen.

Despite being surrounded by so much of hustle bustle and joviality, she was feeling terribly lonely. She desperately looked here and there just to trace signs of compassion somewhere. There were plenty of lewd remarks, suppressed giggles, discordant conversations, and bargaining on offer, but there was hardly anything of the stuff she was looking for—a little sigh of sadness for the departed soul. The odour of wine, cigarettes, betel cones, cheap perfume and flowers permeated everywhere but there was hardly a drop of tear in anyone's eyes. Was a whore's life so unwanted and despicable? Didn't she deserve either a sigh or a few drops of tears?

She had a glimpse of the unwanted and meaningless life even she herself had been living. Had she died in place of Champa, the brothel would have been bustling with crowd unruffled like a cattle market.

Minu cried. However, she didn't know why she was crying. She felt that one day or the other she would also die. Her body would be lying somewhere in some deserted place. Someone, displaying a little kindness, might throw it in a cremation ground, or someone else might sell it to the human-organ dealer. For a moment Minu thought that Champa was more fortunate than her. At least, she herself and Nabaghana were concerned about Champa. When it came to her own, she didn't think anyone would be bothered.

This meaninglessness of life was chasing her like a terrifying spirit. Her childhood, adolescence and youth—all seemed worthless. She realized that she had no one to call her own. Her life was like a handful of sand in an invisible palm. Unknown to her, the sand of life was slipping off. In tune with the slipping sand, she was inching closer to death. The moment that she spent now, in the company of the retreating star in the sky, was just like the night jasmine that had slipped off from its stalk. It would never return to the tree. The day all the sand slipped off, she would die. Her unwanted dead body would be lying in some deserted place. It would be lying unattended, surrounded by jackals and vultures.

All of a sudden, the prospect of life appeared to her very alluring. Earlier, never ever had life appeared so charming and worthwhile. Inwardly, she dreaded death. This dread stemmed out of the suspicion that her body might lie deserted in the cremation ground.

Minu was disgruntled with the brothel. She felt annoyed with Badadei, Malati, Laxmi, Savitri, Pranakrushna, and even, Nabaghana. There was a colony at a distance beyond the boundary wall and the drain. Minu grew jealous of the inhabitants of the colony including the females and the children. How worried the females were about the children ! Disarmed, she sat with her eyes downcast.

At that time, a fair old man lifted the curtain of Minu's room and entered. He had wobbling feet. Betel juice ran down from the corners of his mouth to stain his tidy *Kurta* at a couple of places. In order to attract the attention of Minu, he cleared his throat and spoke in his stentorian voice, "Excuse me ! May I come in?"

Mini gazed at the man. He was around fifty. His tummy bulged and two eyes appeared blood shot.

Minu didn't respond; she remained mum. The man was sexually excited. He just wished to pounce on Minu, just as one flung himself into the swimming pool. He moved a little forward.

Minu wiped tears from her eyes. The withered face of Champa covered in a shawl flashed in her thought. The breeze made the shawl flutter. Any moment the shawl might be removed and the smiling face of Champa, shining like moon, might be exposed.

But how pathetic the face of the waning moon appeared ! How pitiably that lusterless moon shone !

Minu was unable to divert her attention away from the world of tears and sobs, from the funeral pyre, from the winnowing fans, pots and skulls lying scattered in the cremation ground, from Champa's dead body lying in a bundle, unattended at the hospital. She realized that everything else in life —the flower, the bed, the money she earned-- was only an illusion.

Her eyes burnt with sparks of disbelief and disdain. The man however stood unmoved. He took out another cigarette from his pocket and murmured something while lighting it.

Minu got up and taking the man by surprise, took off all her clothes, leaving her completely nude. She took such a little time to undress herself that the man hardly got the opportunity to shut the door or switch off the light.

Minu had several scar marks left by wounds all over her body. The flesh on the left thigh appeared severely scalded at one place. The flabbergasted man looked at Minu first and then one more time towards outside, and fled. Minu shut the door with a thud, switched off the lights and lay on the bed. She could hear the footsteps of the person running down the stairs. Perhaps he thought she was mad and therefore considered it prudent to escape instantly.

In the room, there existed darkness and a nude Minu. Her tears and sighs too. Didn't a whore have the freedom to mourn the death of an acquaintance? Didn't she deserve a little loneliness to cry her heart out? Was she only a doll of flesh and blood, an object of enjoyment? How could someone play with her whenever and wherever he wished? No one bothered whether she had just returned from the cremation ground or after a brush with death or after an accident.

Minu got up exactly at five. A terrible nightmare had disturbed her sleep. She was returning by the market road. Suddenly, that *batiskala* exorcist's eyes fell on her. He had a red hot spatula in his hand. He was followed by Damodar. Both of them gave her a hot pursuit. She ran through the crowd to save her life. Her feet bled as she ran on thorns, pebbles and bricks, for her life. The articles she was carrying fell down and got scattered all around.

Sleep eluded Minu's eyes. She got up, put on her clothes and came to the verandah. There was no one to be seen. Usually, no one got up at that time. By the time they all got up, it would be at least ten. In some inner chamber, the fans whirled. The noise they produced was submerged by the loud roar of the sea. Minu walked up to the stairs noiselessly and clambered up to the terrace.

The sea was clearly visible from the terrace. Only two coconut trees and a tall building in front posed a barrier. The municipal lights were still on. The surrounding looked hazy. The sky above the sea was overshadowed by patches of clouds. Carrying water vapour from the surface of the sea, they were beginning protracted flights. Huge waves rose from the surface. From a distance, it looked as if a caravan of camels was getting up and sitting down alternatively. In that hazy surrounding, the street-lights appeared like lanterns of bullock cart riders approaching from a distance.

The cool morning breeze, blowing into her saree, blouse, bra, petticoat and inner wear, spread all over her body to erase all her weariness, evil thoughts and fear. The presence of a tremendous power wiped away all sense of dread from her mind and made her fearless and relaxed. Minute water particulates, carried by the breeze, moistened her body. With her eyes closed, she experienced their passionate embrace.

The sea was roaring. A hem of Minu's saree started fluttering in the gust of wind. Minu was finding it difficult to re-arrange it. She felt as if someone was adroitly disrobing her. Restlessly, she kept gazing at the sea.

There was no one on the shore. She would have reached there and taken a walk. She was afraid she might be detected by an acquaintance. Over the last few days she kept feeling that she had been noticed and that she was no more able to conceal herself. Once again, she was going to be entangled in an invisible snare.

Who was Minu afraid of? Why? Was she afraid of Damodar? Would Damodar be searching for her even after the lapse of ten years? Why would he be interested in her? A worthless impotent person like him was concerned about only one thing—the recognition of being a married man. He had acquired that recognition years ago. Even after learning that Minu had turned a whore, would he still appear and insist on Minu going back with him?

No, there was no possibility of Damodar looking for her. Who would search for her in that case? Sanatan, Tima or Karuni? Her uncle or aunt? They all lived far away. Fifteen years had elapsed in the meantime. Why would they search for her now? What benefits would they get?

No matter how unwanted and unwelcome she was, Minu knew that only her 'voice' had the right to address her as what she was. She wouldn't be able to accept another person addressing her as a whore. It was more difficult to put up with being addressed as a whore than living like a whore. It was difficult to accept being addressed as an evil-spirit. She wouldn't be able to endure the denunciation and infamy anymore. She was happy with the life she led. There was no need of any other identity. No need at all.

She was born one day. She has to die on another day. The despicable life that she led now was a stage in between life and death. Her life was more a bundle of sighs than anything else. Her life was more worthless and futile than the dust on the road. What was the purpose behind her birth? What difference it would have made to others had she not been born? How would the cruel destiny been impacted?

Minu reminisced through her past. How pathetically she had spent those days ! How every morning and every night she was presented with warm tears and sighs ! She was abused and exploited again and again. However, she had never thought of giving up her life. She kept herself alive.

How attractive life was ! That attraction for life brought her back from the threshold of death again and again. However, she hardly understood why life didn't display compassion and carry her to the doorstep of dignity and possibility. Why did it subject her to one agony after another, one sorrow after another?

Over the last ten years, Minu had contributed to the breaking down of many families. Intentionally, she would detain her customers…till late hours. If her own world was devastated, let their worlds crumble to dust, one by one. Who bothered?

Minu realized that the consolation and encouragement

that had impelled her earlier, returned to her as complaints. More often than not, she had become a victim and not a victor. Her body and soul were battered in the process.

The desire for personal satisfaction had made her deranged. She had ruined many families. Just as the wild waves dismantle sand castles on the shore, so did she ruin many families. At the corner of those ruined houses, with their heads drooping, stood women like her, helplessly. They pointed their fingers at her and cursed her.

The hurt that she had caused to others as Minu, returned to her and hurt her womanhood. The revenge that she wished to exact by becoming a whore boomeranged and wounded her personality. All her blows returned to her, with harsher intensity and more severity.

This feeling almost made Minu crazy. The veins on her forehead swelled and throbbed. Despite the cold breeze of the morning, drops of sweat appeared on her forehead.

Shattering the dreams of others can never restore one's own shattered dreams. If one breaks another's heart, his own broken heart can never be repaired. The success in ruining the home of others can hardly make one forget the failure of shielding one's own home from ruins.

Why did she take shelter there then? Was she alive only for the sake of it? Was she alive for her sustenance? Or, was it because she didn't have the courage to script her death? What was the meaning of the compulsions that regulated her life?

She gazed at her palms. A sense of desperation haunted her. She visualized a small child of five sitting on the bed in front of her. Minu brought a comb, some oil, powder and *kajal*. She applied oil to the child's hair and combed it. She dabbed his face with powder; she applied *kajal* in the middle of his forehead. At the sight of his appearance, her heart was filled with love. She dragged the child towards her, put him in her lap and rubbed his face with hers. Putting him on her bosom, she planted hundreds of kisses on his shoulder, back, feet, and palms. Dreading that someone might cast his evil eyes on him, she smeared a little bit of *kajal* just below his chin.

Minu got back to her senses. No, that cute little child wasn't there with her. This was only a pillow. She didn't have a child of her own. If she had one, it would have taken birth shattering her entrails, leaving her bathing in blood, rendering her crumpled, exhausted and senseless. It would have transported her back from her senseless state with its childish cries. Her entire life was spent like a waterless summer. She was reduced to a dry piece of barren land and left abandoned.

What worth such a life had ! She picked up the pillow and flung it far away from there.

Nabaghana had been waiting for quite some time to talk to her. At the sight of her solemn appearance, he hesitated to say anything. Many people visited the brothel. Even, some of the girls would travel to hotels to entertain their customers. Nabaghana would make fun of those girls at times. However, he couldn't muster courage to make fun of Minu. In her very presence, he would flinch with fear.

While arranging the crumpled bedsheet, Minu looked at Nabaghana and said, "What do you want?'

Nabaghana mustered courage to enter inside. Since the death of Champa, he had marked many changes in Minu. Especially because of that, his nervousness and fear for her had deepened. There were so many others in the brothel. Badadei had no dearth of money with her. However, none of them wished to go to the cremation ground. Thinking that they would have to be embroiled in a police case if they went there, they shirked their responsibilities. Had she wished, Minu could have stayed away from the trouble of cremating Champa. How was Champa related to her? Was she her sister? No. Still then, she carried her body from the hospital and cremated it. The next morning, she visited the cremation ground to pick up her bone from the ashes to consign those in the sea. She shed tears, she prayed God for her. Was it worth nothing?

Nabaghana talked many times to himself as to who this Minu was. Where had she come from? He had seen her from the day he came to the brothel. With the passage of time, she had become more and more mysterious to him. He had miserably failed to solve the mystery. Many types of girls reached the brothel at different points in time. Most of them were cheap and worthless. They would speak nonsense. They had detestable dressing manners. Like the trapeze artists of a circus, they roamed here and there throughout the day. With the dab of powder and lipstick, they appeared more repulsive than appealing. They were concerned with only one thing—how to earn more money. The thought of ornaments, expensive clothes drove them crazy. They behaved like they had no other concern in life.

How did Minu manage herself in the company of such shameless creatures? Nabaghana indulged in such speculations during his leisure time but he hardly got any answers. He only guessed that Minu must have been crushed by insurmountable grief. Perhaps without any solution at sight, she stuck to this place.

Nabaghana said, "Badadei is looking for you. Please go and meet her when you are free."

"You can leave. I'll go after completing some tasks."

Nabaghana went away. After arranging her saree, Minu looked outside through the window. Pranakrushna was getting down his office jeep and coming towards the brothel. He was in uniform.

What brought him to the brothel so early in the morning? Whose death message did he carry now? Minu's heart started beating faster at such thoughts.

When in his police uniform, Pranakrushna would never come to the first floor. He would sit in the guest room on the ground floor and summon whoever he wanted. On the other hand, when he was to directly enter Minu's room on the first floor to spend his entire time there, he would come soberly dressed in his civilian garb.

Even though she had received no summons, Minu came down to the ground floor. If the officer carried any bad news, she should know it as soon as possible. Waiting to be informed by someone else was a mere torture.

On seeing Minu he said, I'm here on an enquiry. Where is the owner?'

While receiving him with folded hands, Badadei said, "Please take a seat, Sir. Had you informed me, I would have come to the police station. You…" Without completing the sentence she told Minu, "Minu, go and ask Nabaghana to get a glass of cold water for Sir."

Pranakrushna interjected, "No need of that. I am in a great hurry. A young girl has been missing for seven days. There is no trace of her. Police have registered a case. We are suspicious about the involvement of your brothel. Be careful. If you try to hide anything, you'll land in trouble. I have come to warn you."

Badadei spoke in a quivering voice, "No, Sir. No girl has come here. If she comes, I'll surely bring it to your notice. Here, we never promote any illegal activities…"

"Stop ! You don't need to tell me anything about that," said Pranakrushna without allowing Badadei to complete her sentence. Then he got up from the chair. Minu courteously took a few steps after him. When he reached the jeep, he turned back and told Minu, "I have some business with you. I'll meet you in the evening."

The jeep left with Pranakrushna. Minu turned back. Badadei's face reflected a horror. Was the girl with her, then? Did she tell a lie to Pranakrushna?

Minu could read another reflection from Badadei's face. Badadei was unable to digest the fact that Pranakrushna appreciated Minu more than her. Minu cast her eyes downwards. Badadei said, "Minu ! Will you please come to my room?" She replied, "Yes, after some time."

Minu waited for Pranakrushna that evening. Her anxieties deepened for three specific reasons. She was feeling restless over the last few days and wished to speak her heart out to someone. Secondly, she wished to know more about the unfortunate girl who had been abducted and if she had been abandoned at the brothel. She felt restless to know what the important business was that Pranakrushna wished to share with her.

After a hearty lunch, she took a nap. Sleep eluded her during the nights. So, she felt like compensating it with a nap during the day. She was reminded of Badadei's summon. She went there unwillingly. Almost every day she would tell her the same thing. The business was on a decline. On the other hand, exploitation by the police, municipality and excise staff was on the rise. How would they manage with so many encumbrances?

Minu didn't have answers to such questions. She didn't know why Badadei wished to discuss business matters only with her when there were so many others. What could a person like her, who had lived a meaningless life and who had been shown the door by the entire world for being worthless, do to help her? Surprisingly, Badadei trusted Minu's abilities. Since the day she had reached here in a helpless state, she took a great deal of interest in the day to day affairs at the brothel. Every inhabitant praised her intellect and efficiency.

Such trust in her abilities was not entirely misplaced. If a person, who didn't have anything worthwhile to do, was offered some job, he would do with his heart in it. He would engage himself day in and day out in the job and ensure that it was done properly. The same was the case with Minu. She took great delight in associating herself with the normal day to day affairs. Whether it were profits and losses, tidying up activities or repairs, she always took the lead.

Whether Minu was genuinely interested in organizing the brothel or she deliberately kept herself busy seeking respite from her troubled past ! Only she knew.

Minu wasn't interested in any such thing anymore. Her life had gone out of track and there was little possibility of bringing it back. She no more indulged in such thoughts. She wished the days should pass; she should sleep one night, never to get up again.

Badadei said, "These days, Munsif Mian has a bad mood most of the time. He feels irritated. Almost every month, he incurs a loss. He wants new 'items'."

Minu got up suddenly. She would have no opinion in this regard. Many young girls had spoiled their lives by coming here. She wouldn't be able to tolerate a repetition of that. No matter how one felt, she would never support any such move. Look at what happened to Champa, her dead body lay by the side of a drain like an orphan's. Despite knowing all this, how Badadei dared bring another girl to an irrecoverable state of ruins.

"Minu, life is never meant to be easy. It subjects one to several tests. Who will visit the brothel if young girls aren't periodically inducted into it?"

Minu was filled with disdain and helplessness. Badadei was right. Like all others, this was also a business. Just as in a showroom, one had to stock fresh products along with old ones, the same was the case here. She was only a product to be displayed before the customers. In the past, she was in great demand and therefore sold at a higher price. With the passage of time, there had been a decline in her price. One day, she would become old and worn out. No customer would take liking for her. It's immaterial to think what would happen to her then. But how would the brothel run?

"Munsif Mian has arranged a new one for the brothel. You should train her."

Minu remained mum. Badadei spoke, "This Sunday evening, Munsif Mian and his friends would arrive. What would I do? I am born with an ill-fate. There is no escape from the abuses of others."

Minu had met Munsif Mian on a couple of occasions earlier. At the thought of him, she shivered in dread. He was a demon. Most of the time, he was found carrying a pistol and a knife. He was the owner of this brothel. Minu wasn't interested in the details of chilling testimonies about him but she was well-aware that he was a dreadful beast.

Badadei spoke, "Minu, think over it. That young girl is expected to arrive tomorrow. Your duty is to prepare her for the job. Do that, otherwise we all will be in trouble." Badadei got up and went away.

Minu felt as if Badadei had issued veiled threats to her. Her statement clearly indicated that Minu might invite the ire of some and face serious consequences if she didn't do as desired.

Minu grew afraid. If she was expelled from the brothel, what would she do? Where would she go? The world had no place for one who had lived in a brothel. No one would offer her refuge; people would feel ashamed even to look in her direction. Those who were expressing compassion for her ill-fate now would turn their faces away very soon.

The strange experiences concerning life worried Minu. She didn't harbour the desire to continue living here. On the other hand, there was no hope of going away. Even if she went away, there was no hope of getting refuge anywhere. All of them living there were like helpless creatures facing a blind alley. Their lives were no better than that of worms in a gutter.

Minu felt terrible anger and frustration seizing her. She strode back to her room. She threw away the clothes lying scattered on the bed and flung herself on it with her face buried in the pillow.

Minu dreamed in her sleep. The music of a band party playing somewhere nearby reached her ears. Lights dazzled up the atmosphere. People danced merrily. The entire place was decorated with flowers. A bridegroom sat in a decorated car. He was followed by his companions. They all came and gathered in front of Minu's house. The bride's side welcomed the groom and his party.

Someone came and whispered something into Minu's ears. Minu wasn't able to hear her as the noise of bands and crackers deafened her. She asked loudly what the matter was.

The girl standing nearby shrugged and repeated what she had told earlier.

Someone knocked on the door. Minu's sleep broke. The room was enveloped in darkness. A strange stench emanated from somewhere. She got up and arranged her clothes. She switched on the lights. She removed the curtain and unlatched the door.

Pranakrushna was standing outside, no one knew for how long. The moment his eyes fell on Minu he said, "Were you asleep? I had some important business with you. That's why…"

Minu remembered. Pranakrushna had informed her in the morning that he would visit her in the evening. Only she had forgotten. She said, "Please come in."

Pranakrushna was not in his uniform. He wore a cotton Punjabi and a *chudidar*. He seemed extremely happy.

Minu burnt two incense sticks. A delicate fragrance spread through the room. In one corner of the room, she had placed the photos of Gods. She went there, tucked the incense sticks in the holder and came back to him.

Pranakrushna said, "I've some good news for you."

A ray of smile appeared on Minu's face, dispelling her gloomy appearance. What good news did he carry for her? What good news she waited for these days ! The time for waiting for good news was over long back. What good can she expect now?

Pranakrushna had something wrapped in a small packet. He had held it hidden at his back. He brought his hand forward and displayed the packet to Minu. It contained *ladoos*. Minu was surprised. Was he promoted?

Pranakrushna said, "Take this. Eat it up, I say."

Minu picked up a *ladoos*. Pranakrushna was really happy. Something that had seemed impossible for long had become possible. His wife had decided to return. When all his hopes had been shattered and he had reached the conclusion that divorce was the last resort, his wife understood her mistake and decided to come back.

"I'm very happy that she has decided to return." Pranakrushna's usual harsh appearance as a policeman underwent a transformation while giving her the information.

He appeared bashful like a young man of twenty. The feeling of joy was conspicuous on his face.

Minu heaved a sigh of relief. Her eyes welled up. Was it in joy or sorrow? Was she happy that the discord between husband and wife had been amicably resolved? Did she feel agonized at the prospect of losing Pranakrushna forever? Was her heart tormented at her inability to erase the fissure in her own life, or she was jealous and envious as someone else's family was going to be set up once again while her own ended in a failure? She didn't know.

Pranakrushna was eager to get up and go. She didn't try to detain him any longer. Over the last few years, her intimacy with him had grown deeper. Minu never thought of what he had got from her. He had given her a sense of protection, compassion and friendship.

"You please leave now. I'm very happy for you. I lead an ignoble life. Otherwise, I would have gone there personally and accorded her a warm welcome."

He was going to say something but stopped in the middle. What would he have said? Did someone invite a whore home? Besides, as a police officer it was his duty to prevent prostitution. How would he then honour one by inviting her home?

Pranakrushna said, "I want to say you something. Please don't misunderstand me."

Minu raised her head and said, "No...no...have I ever misunderstood you?"

"Please leave this place and go away. If you wish, I can make an effort to help you."

Minu shuddered. She had never thought that someone could advise her to leave the place forever. She shuddered as the same Pranakrushna, who had approved of her presence in the brothel was asking her to leave it today.

Minu cast her look downwards once again. Pranakrushna's suggestion made her past life seem more contemptible and worthless. It's true that he had been able to re-establish his family. He would no more need to be a guest at a brothel. There was a time, however, when the attraction of the brothel was too difficult for him to resist. He put his position, honour and dignity at stake and arrived here. However, every Pranakrushna in the world was not able to reach a settlement in his disturbed family. The wife of one Pranakrushna had returned to him bringing an end to his need of visiting the brothel. But, the others were still there. Every year new Pranakrushnas joined the group of earlier ones.

Minu said, "Thank you. Let you never feel the need to visit this hell ! Where would I go? For me, all doors of the society are closed, the confines of this hell are much better."

"But..."

"These ifs and buts have no meaning. Thank you for your concern and compassion. I am sorry I can't go by your advice."

Minu reached the door ahead of him and held it open. Pranakrushna understood the implicit message. He turned and went away. The noise of his footsteps on the stairs receded in the distance.

Minu shut the door and returned to the bed. She felt like crying. For the first time, she wasn't able to find the reason for shedding tears.

Pranakrushna's proposal rang in her mind time and again. A sense of dread enveloped her. Was she being turned out of her refuge? Were layers after layers of her personality being peeled off in broad daylight?

Where would she go? Who would accept her? Wherever she went, people would ask her questions about her past. What would she answer? In the pretext of displaying compassion, they would dig deep into her and try to find out what she did to make a living. Not only one or two but hundreds of them would prick her body and soul with the same question. They would ask for a price for providing refuge. Would she be able to withstand such humiliation?

For the first time, Minu's eyes were moistened by a sense of affection for the brothel. In comparison to the pitiless world outside, the untidy and lusty atmosphere seemed more intimate. No one forced her to leave this place; no one pestered her with questions against her wishes. Here, her life wasn't considered worthless. She didn't have to bend down before someone for his sympathy. She didn't have to beg for people's kindness or compassion either.

She would stay here. Every one like Pranakrushna hadn't been able to mend the broken threads and re-established a connect. If one family was restored, there were five more which disintegrated. In place of one Pranakrushna, there would be five more. The brothel would exist to provide them succor. So long as tears, sobs, wrath, pride, and weal and woe of these unfortunate ones existed, Minu could never be exterminated. She would continue to exist.

Pranakrushna had gone away. With his departure, the possibility of meeting him grew feeble. All of a sudden Minu felt that she had grown more intimate with him and considered him her own. Otherwise, why should she have experienced grief at his departure? Why did she feel as if her heart had been emptied of something?

Intense relationships leave a void when they break. The relationships that cause joy when established cause an equal heartburn when they end. The deeper the roots go, the more difficult it becomes to pull them out.

Who had asked Minu to barter her heart away to Pranakrushna? No one visited the brothel seeking her love. The customers came seeking the pleasure of her body. They paid for what they sought. The price depended on the time consumed and pleasure obtained. No one paid for the sake of Minu's emotions or for the sake of her love.

Minu made herself firm. She had to live here, in this brothel. There was no alternative for her. She had no one to call her own. She would stay here instead of going to any orphanage.

A drop of tear appeared at one corner of her eye. It was going to run off and wipe away the line of *kajal*. It was about to render Minu's cheeks and lips lusterless. She controlled her breathing in order to stem its flow. She held the corner of her saree and wished it to soak the teardrop.

However, it was too late by then. The helpless tear had descended from the eye.

Minu sat down, exhausted. Feeling angry and hapless, she wiped the powder clean from her cheeks. She plucked the garland from her chignon and crushed it. Let everything be wiped, let everything be broken and destroyed.

Thursdays and *sankranti* days are considered holy by the Hindus. Despite being subjected to so much torture and abuse, there was no decline in Minu's devotion for Gods. This faith had stuck to her heart like a solid stone under the stairs. She had great reverence for occasions like *purnami, amavasya, ekadasi* and *sankranti.* On those occasions, she would try her best to stay away from wine and chicken. At times, her efforts would end in failure. How much freedom a subservient whore was expected to enjoy ! Her fasting and maintaining vows would meet a premature end at times.

Today, she got up and emerged from the brothel early. After taking a walk along the beach, she reached the bazzar. She didn't have to do much shopping. It's true that all the people who come to the bazzar don't come for shopping. Shopping for her was only an excuse. Minu needed to be aloof; she needed respite for a couple of hours.

A girl was buying a hand-crafted doll and a chain from a shop to the left. She was around fifteen or sixteen. She appeared charming and had chubby cheeks. She had put on a saree with a coordinated sequence of pink and green. The stone-studded chain shone in her hand.

Minu forgot her troubles for a moment. The girl's mother stood by her. She was no more than Minu's age. A deep sigh emerged from Minu's heart and disappeared. If she had borne a girl, she would have been of this child's age.

When the girl turned her face towards Minu, the latter cast her eyes downwards. To cast glances at someone surreptitiously was discourteous. The feeling of guilt shrank her within. The girl went away after buying the chain.

Minu raised her head and looked up. The shop attendant was arranging the chains in their place on the shelf. He had to display a large number of chains just to sell one.

When her eyes fell on the face of the man, she stood thunderstruck for a moment. She felt as if the world under her feet was crumbling. She hurried away from the spot.

The corner of Minu's saree stuck to the hood of a rickshaw. When she pulled at it, it got torn. However, Minu wasn't concerned about that. She continued walking ahead. She felt as if someone was tugging at her saree from behind.

But, who was it?

It was Karuni.

The eight or nine year old boy at the rehearsal hall had turned a sturdy young man. She had scurried away from the spot but she decided to return. She went to the bangle and chain shop and stood there silently.

Karuni said, "Should I show you bangles?"

Minu couldn't reply. The sobs jostled with each other to gush out. Not a word emerged from her mouth.

Karuni felt startled when his eyes fell on her.

He yelled, "Minudei !" Restraining her tears and sobs, Minu shook her head and said, "Yes dear, it's me."

Karuni left his shop and came out. He bent down to touch her feet. Minu quickly retreated and said, "Don't touch me, don't touch. If you touch my feet I'll incur sin?"

Minu gazed at Karuni. Their village, surrounded by tamarind, *chakunda* and bamboo groves, stood far away. Many years ago, this boy would roam around the rehearsal hall for hours, with a few cups without holders on them. That was this Karuni.

Surprise was writ large in Karuni's eyes, "How come you are here?"

Minu's eyes reflected inquisitiveness, "Since when have you been working here?"

The questions however remained unasked. How could someone narrate the incidents spanning so many years in a few words? Would the incidents flash before the eyes, like in a film?

Karuni said, "Please wait for some time. Let me down the shutters. We'll go to my place."

Minu sought a little isolation. She wasn't feeling comfortable in the market. She dreaded that someone might recognize her. The revelation of her present identity would shatter Karuni's sense of respect for her.

Karuni went away to down the shutters. Minu was busy contemplating if she had done the right thing by appearing so suddenly before Karuni. She had spent so many years in self-exile. What compelled her to appear before an acquaintance and reveal her identity?

The memories of the past clung to her. She found it difficult to release her from their grip.

Karuni returned. His face reflected his worry. He said, "Please come with me, Minudei. My residence is on the next turn."

About twenty meters away from the spot, towards the left, ran a lane. Towards its right, there was an alley. Karuni opened a tin gate and said, "Come in, Minudei."

Karuni closed the gate and followed Minu. There was a room with an asbestos roof at the back of a pucca building. It was locked. Karuni unlocked the door and went inside. He opened the window and arranged the clothes lying scattered on a string bed.

"Please have a sit here, Minudei. Let me go out for a minute."

Karuni's worry melted Minu. What sort of relationship did they share? Both of them were only neighbours in the same village. He wasn't born of the same mother. Those whom she considered her own didn't care for her at all. Despite not belonging to her family, how much Karuni was worried for her !

Karuni returned with four *samosas* and two sweet cakes in a leaf bowl. He took out an aluminium plate from under the string bed and kept the items on it. He poured some water into a glass from the earthen pot and said, "Minudei, please eat some."

Flashing a smile Minu said, "Today is *ekadashi,* a holy day. I won't eat all this stuff. You eat. Let me sit here and watch you."

Karuni's worries knew no bound. He said, "Let me go and bring some bananas and apples for you."

Minu responded, "There is no need. Sit down. I'll manage with a sweet."

"In that case, you take both the sweets."

"Okay, okay."

While stuffing his mouth with a *samosa,* Karuni said, "Tell me something about you first."

Minu sighed deeply. She drank a little water from the glass and said, "Please tell me something about you first. I had some news about Gangadhar Sir. Tell me what Sukadev is doing these days."

Karuni became solemn. "Why should I make you sad by telling all this? When you were still living in the village, his wife left for her father's place, never to return again. He is into some business at Kolkatta. He has no relationship with the other members of his family back in the village. He visited the village only once during the obsequies rituals of his father."

"Ratnakar uncle passed away !"

"Yes, he passed away some eight years ago."

Minu broke down. She felt as if a burning lamp was suddenly extinguished. She leaned onto the wall and sighed.

"After you departed, your uncle took possession of the homestead land. He grew brinjals there. He would often call you names on some pretext or the other."

"But why? What wrong have I done to him?"

"He was angry with you as you abandoned your father-in-law's place."

"Leave it. Tell me, what are Tima bhai and Sura bhai doing these days?"

'Tima bhai suffered from Tuberculosis. By the time he went to the hospital, his condition had grown serious. He is taking medicines, no doubt, but is living a hellish life."

Two drops of tear rolled down her cheeks. The figure of a handsome young man flashed before her eyes. Such a young man, how could he contract T.B.?

"Sura bhai was always crazy. How could he give up his love for singing? With the passage of time, his family expanded. After he had three daughters, his mother started creating trouble for his wife. He left the village with his children and is living in a brick-kiln somewhere in Cuttack. I haven't met him for years."

Minu had lost her patience to hear anything more. Had she returned to Karuni's shop to hear all these? Had she nurtured the memories of all these years fondly, only to hear this? Why did these people undergo so much suffering?

Really, she was an evil spirit. How could a person, who had grown acquaintance with her, live in peace?

A feeling of guilt moistened her eyes. Karuni went on narrating one incident after another relating to the village. "Kirtan has opened a coaching centre and is teaching children. The rehearsal hall has turned a haunted den."

"Haunted den !"

"Your uncle, Sukadev's father and a few others arrived there one evening to dismantle it. Suddenly, a ghost appeared from nowhere and chased them. They ran away from the spot in great dread. Since then, they haven't stepped there another time."

"Are you telling the truth?'

"For God's sake, Minudei. The roof wasn't thatched for years. The roof along with the beams supporting it collapsed. Now the whole thing has turned to an ant-hill. The inhabitants of your village report that at times, during the night, dhol and harmonium sounds emanate from the place. I have never heard it though…"

Despite being affected by so much grief, Karuni's innocence made Minu burst out to a laugh. He hadn't changed at all.

Karuni continued his description for a long time. He drank a little water from the glass and said, "What are you doing here, Minudei? We all thought…"

"I had died… didn't you think so?" Minu cut in.

Thinking that his eyes might meet that of Minu, a guilty Karuni looked outside.

Minu got up. She said, "During this period, I have lived my life no doubt, but it is as good as death. You may take it as you please. For my sake, Karuni, don't tell anyone that you had met me. I'll come here the next Monday and narrate you everything."

Karuni was not ready to be satisfied with Minu's request. He got up and said, "For my sake, Minudei…we have met after so many years…please tell me where are you living and what you are doing."

Minu felt confounded. What'll she say? What was her identity? She could never reveal the truth.

In order to circumvent Karuni's question she said, "Tell me…since when have you opened the shop here? How is your business doing? Have you got married or not?"

Karuni replied, "Stop asking so many questions at one go. How can I answer all these at the same time? I opened the shop six months ago. Regarding my marriage…"

"What?"

"Arrangements are being made. Won't I send a message to you?"

Despite suffering, the bashful Karuni's words made Minu happy. Like a sister she said, "Hmm ! Had I died, I would have taken birth somewhere else by now. How could you have passed the message then?"

Karuni remained mum.

Minu came outside. She said, "No need of accompanying me. I'll visit the temple before leaving for my residence."

Karuni didn't accept the suggestion. He said, "Let's go together. I'll arrange a rickshaw for you and then return."

Karuni arranged a rickshaw for her at the end of the lane. Minu pulled her veil further. If someone recognized her when Karuni was present, she would be ashamed. She wouldn't be able to show him her face again.

She had never felt as disoriented about her identity as she did that day. She wished to go as far away from Karuni as was possible. She wished to be at an unreachable distance from him.

Suddenly, a police jeep passed by her. Minu's heart started beating faster apprehending danger. Thank God, no one had seen her.

The moment she climbed onto the seat of the rickshaw, she asked the rickshaw-puller to raise the hood.

The rickshaw-puller started negotiating through an inclining road.

The moment she reached the brothel, she hurried into her room and shut the door. She dreaded that someone might be following her. Once inside, she felt light and breathed comfortably. When she had left the brothel in the morning, she thought of spending the entire day outside and returning only in the evening. But to her surprise it was only midday.

Minu gazed at the sea through the window. The dazzling sun played on the surface of the sea like a playful child hanging onto his father's back. Far away the gentle waves glistened.

Since the time she had met Karuni, she felt as if something was getting ripped to shreds within her. Those who had remained alive and fresh in her memory so long suddenly turned old and incapacitated. Those who were beautiful and attractive suddenly turned ugly and repelling.

How charming the portrayals in her memory were! She relished those while she was away from them. She had abandoned her village, her uncle's home, her in-laws, the rehearsal hall and all friends that she had made while working there. She hoped everything would have fallen back into place. Rehearsals would be going on in the rehearsal hall. The single-roomed house would be reverberating with the sounds of *dhols* and harmonium.

However, nothing of that sort had happened. Things never went the way Minu dreamed. Rather, they had their own way of taking divergent paths. How could Minu's suffering aggravate, otherwise?

An unmarried young lady cried out in distress within her. She was busy searching for the fragments of her memory. She wished to rearrange everything immaculately and bring them back to their former shape.

She was now worried about the village that had given her nothing but disgrace. She craved for its groves, ponds, school field, rehearsal hall and the childhood she had spent there.

Surprisingly, she found two invisible and strong shackles confining her to a peg. She realized that she would never be able to reach the village breaking the shackles or defying the restraints imposed by the peg.

Karuni had put it right. She had died. Unknown to her, she had died long ago.

Minu decided to remain firm. She collected all her emotions and concerns, made a bundle of those and threw it away. If she was as good as dead for the people of the village, the village was no different for her. Relationships could not be one-sided. She had to live with whatever was left in her life. No matter how base and unwanted it was, she had to live with it. The tears, the sobs, the exploitations and the abuses were all but hers. She would live with all of it.

Minu lay on the bed. A storm raged inside her. If she didn't control herself, it would blow her away.

Minu got up after some time. She headed towards the corner where, on a wooden plank, she had placed the photos of gods and goddesses. With her head touching the wall, she beseeched, "O God ! Give me the strength to bear everything."

Minu shuddered at the thought of some mishap the moment she saw Param Mondal. Some calamity or the other always accompanied him. There was hardly any correlation between his words and his actions. His words were always sugar-coated. He would always behave intimately with everyone. But, he was a well-wisher of none. Minu often doubted if he was honest with himself.

People like Mondal were among the patrons of the brothel. They enjoyed a lot of importance. They often put their life at risk for the brothel. They were benefitted in the process no doubt, but there was greater possibility of danger than profits.

Mondal was a pimp. His job involved supplying girls and customers to the brothel. He demanded high commission for his work. The price depended on the quality of the 'item' supplied. His responsibility was confined till he delivered the individual at the doorstep of the brothel. He wasn't responsible for any eventuality thereafter.

Minu was eager to know what Mondal was doing there so early in the morning.

Mondal reached the brothel. He threw down the cigarette butt and crushed it under his heel. He came upstairs dragging his foot gear. He would go till Badadei's room. Minu ambled till her room.

Mondal tried to explain something to Badadei. Minu eavesdropped their conversation.

"Who had told you to do such a thing?" a worried Badadei was heard asking.

"But this 'item' is extraordinarily attractive," replied Mondal.

"I understand, but if the police file a case, you'll be sent to jail. I'll be dragged there too. Moreover, that bastard inspector is causing much trouble."

"How would the police know? When they come to know after a fortnight or so, the 'item' would have grown old in the field. Who'll take her back then? Even her own people will desert her." Mondal gave a mischievous smile while saying so.

"How stupid you are ! Badadei lost her temper. I had told you to convince her before bringing her here. There was no problem if you had to pay extra bucks for that. Why did you tell her lies and…"

"Please listen to me. Allow me to speak. She needed a job. She is educated. I found that it was easy to convince her. The moment I said that I would arrange a suitable job for her she immediately agreed…"

"No…no. There are huge risks involved. Besides, that inspector frequents this place. There'll be trouble for sure."

"There is nothing to be afraid of. She'll understand everything in a day or two. Besides, have you calculated the profits you can pocket every month?"

Badadei perked up. The possibility of a huge profit delighted her. Keeping her joy under wraps, she said, "Don't try to flatter me."

"Let me take your leave, Badadei. Munsif Mian will arrive here on Sunday evening. Please mind what I said."

Badadei was about to come outside to spit out her

betel juice. Minu hurriedly left the place. By now she was aware that Mondal had used his crooked ways to get hold of another girl. Munsif Mian will arrive on Sunday evening to rape her.

Oh God ! Minu uttered these words and returned to her room. She grew compassionate towards the unknown girl.

But, what could Minu do? It was easy to get an entry to the brothel, but very difficult to find a way out. Munsif Mian had employed pimps and goons to keep an eye on everybody. They all were terrible monsters. Even if one would hide in hell, they would drag him out.

Why was Minu so much worried about the whole issue? Was something novel going to happen? In the past, many young girls had been brought here. Some of them protested vehemently for the first couple of weeks. Later, either compelled by circumstances or in greed for money, they all gave in and accepted their fate.

'A woman's life is akin to the life of a patch of grass under a boulder. It's full of distressing situations. She has to bank on the compassion, sympathy and kindness of others. Whether at her parents' place, at the destitute home or at the brothel—everywhere she requires compassion and kindness. How dear a life of two square meals a day and a five-hand-saree costs !

A woman's life is similar to that of a snail's. It drags itself ahead. If one kicks the snail away, another one drags it down with a stick. Still another one makes it lie upside down and kicks it on the head. The helpless snail fails to protect itself. It moves on in search of source of water. It spends its entire life in search of refuge in vain.

Today is Saturday. It'll be Sunday tomorrow. Munsif Mian would arrive with a renowned customer. Perhaps some contractor or some officer ! He would treat him to a sumptuous banquet. He would get his work done with the gifts. Munsif Mian had great connections among the officers. His main business was to encroach upon government fallow land, pastures and the low lands beside the road. At first, he would have a fence around the government land. Next, he would have a garage or a *dhaba* constructed there. Gradually, he would get the disputed land registered in his name. He would finally sell it to someone at a premium.

Minu was never interested in all these affairs of Munsif Mian. She only knew that he was a ferocious beast. He believed in defying rules and regulations. Anything that was holy and pious meant nothing for him.

Minu felt extremely wearied. This was exactly how she had felt on the day of her mother's death, after her relationship with the rehearsal hall was snapped, and after tolerating the tortures inflicted by the exorcists. That helplessness had driven her to this place—to this flesh trade where people understood nothing other than gratifying sexual impulses. This was a place where heart, soul and all such considerations had no value at all.

Ten years had gone by in the meantime. The waves had kissed the shore innumerable times before retreating. The sun and moon had risen uncountable times before setting. Her youth had lost its vigour. Her body and mind had become fatigued. She felt as if she had spent an aeon in this discoloured old two-storeyed building.

Minu got up. The new girl was housed in Champa's bedroom. Param Mondal had deceitfully brought her here. On the pretext of arranging a job, he had brought her to this hell. She was the new 'item' of this showroom. She was treated neither as a girl nor a woman nor a human being but an 'item'. Just as people collected potatoes and pumpkin from the greengrocer's, rice and wheat from the grocery shop, similarly customers came to the brothel to enjoy the flesh of the new 'item'. Customers would be attracted towards the new 'item' and enquire for her price. In the meantime, some of the old 'items' would also find customers.

At the sight of that building, Minu felt as if someone had wrapped her in a blanket of aversion and indifference. She would experience the pain of suppressed sobs just below her throat. Her heart would revolt. Poor Champa ! How much she laughed and danced ! What great dreams she had !

The door was closed from outside. Minu seethed in anger. What sort of heartlessness it was ! Was a human being inferior to a goat, sheep or hen? The legs of such animals were tied. They were confined to a room so that they wouldn't escape. Helplessly lying within the four walls, they would be moaning. When needed, they would be butchered. But were human beings like them?

The door produced a creaking noise when it was opened. A ray of sunlight entered the room. A listless girl, barely seventeen, sat leaning against a wall. She didn't even sit on the bed. It looked as if someone had stuck nails on her head that leaned onto one side. It was difficult to gauge from a distance whether she was alive or dead.

Minu quickened her steps. She found a mug containing some water and a glass on the bed. She poured some water into the glass and went near the girl. The girl gazed at her with wide eyes. Minu looked into her face and said, "Drink some water."

The girl drank the water in the glass immediately. She was extremely thirsty. Minu offered her another glass. The girl's clothes were drenched in sweat. Drops of perspiration appeared on her forehead. Minu tried to guess when exactly she had left home. Her shabby clothes indicated that she hadn't changed them for days.

Minu said, "Come and sit near the window. Let me bring some clothes for you. Change into those."

The girl gathered a little courage. Clutching at the feet of Minu, she cried out, "Maa !"

Maa ! Who was the 'Maa'? How could Minu become a 'Maa'? Minu paused a while. She cast her eyes downwards. The girl lay prostrate on the ground clutching onto her feet. She looked like a hapless woman lying prostrate at the feet of the deity.

Minu had heard the word 'Maa' many times in her life. She had heard it in the market, in the bazzar, from the female servant at the brothel and amidst unknown old men and women. But, there it was only a formality of addressing someone. Nothing more than that. Why did the helpless girl's calling her 'Maa' sound different? Why was it making her weak?

Minu was always eager to hear someone address her by that word 'Maa'. Such address had the power to melt her flesh, bones and bone-marrow. Her mind and soul would be filled with the holy waters of affection, an opportunity hitherto denied to her. For a moment she would forget all tortures, abuses and self-effacement. All her dreams would be fulfilled then.

On many an occasion in the past, Minu had dreamt of a small child. She had even kissed him on his tender cheeks. She had dabbed him with *kajal* and powder. She lent ears to his babbling, hoping that he would call him 'Maa'. "Just call me once, my child. Call me 'Maa,' 'Maa,' 'Maa'," she had urged with him many times.

Unfortunately, no one had ever addressed her as

'Maa'. She never had the opportunity to be enchanted by the smell of turmeric paste applied on the body of the child. The sour-smelling lips of no child had ever brushed against her cheeks and chins. Hapless, she spent one night after another.

When Minu thought of the misfortunes in her life, she was reminded of a distressing sight. She was a child then. She lived with her uncle's family at Madhupur. One afternoon, she had gone to the lanes where the low-caste *harijans* lived. She and some of her friends were roaming in the shade under the mango groves.

A swineherd was coming from the opposite side with seven or eight pigs. He was followed by around thirty people. The swineherd paused near a canal. The canal was about to overflow with rain water. After some bargains were made, the swineherd drove the pigs into the canal. The herd flung itself into the water in order to cross the canal.

The swineherd, who was standing on the bank till then, tied a *gamchha* around his waist. He pounced on the last pig that had jumped into the water. He held it by its hind legs. The entire face of the pig including its eyes and nose was drowned in water. It was groaning but the swineherd wasn't ready to allow it any respite. He pulled at it with greater force and got it drowned under water to die.

Minu's entire body shook like tender leaves in the storm. She ran back home and disappeared in her grandmother's lap.

At times, the unfortunate pig appeared before Minu. How many times the pig would have expressed its gratitude to the swineherd thinking that it was he who gave him food! How would the pig understand that no earnest feelings but only sly business instincts guided his master?

Despite the best of her efforts, Minu was never able to erase the memory of that detestable act of drowning the pig in water till its death. She felt as if the number of swineherds was multiplying in this world. On the other hand, the number of innocent pigs was declining.

Minu sat down. The girl was still clutching her legs. Minu asked her, "What's your name?"

"Arundhati."

Softening her voice a bit, she asked again, "What's your problem here? You'll get enough to eat and nice clothes to wear. You'll be granted freedom to do as you wish. There'll be no dearth of pleasure and amusement. Whatever you wish will be made available."

"Please don't tempt me with such talks. I beseech you with folded hands. I fall at your feet, please save me, Maa. My parents must have gone crazy by now. Please save me, Maa. Please allow me respite from here. I'll remain ever grateful to you."

Minu felt as if she would go mad. She could not tolerate distressing cries of the girl. Her inability to protect the one who addressed her as 'Maa' for the first time made her feel helpless.

She sat down and wiped the tears from Arundhati's eyes. She caressed her hair fondly. "Pray to God earnestly. None other than He can help you. Listen carefully to what I say. I'll come once again at night."

Minu left Arundhati behind and locked the door from outside.

How strange, outside there was the bright light of day, and inside the reign of darkness.

After returning from Arundhati's room, Minu became remorseful. She was in a dilemma as to what she could do for her. In most matters related to the brothel, Badadei listened to her advice. But, she would never accede to the request and permit Arundhati to escape. She would grow suspicious and complain that Minu had secretly joined hands with the police.

Had Minu really joined hands with the police? No, she had rejected Pranakrushna's proposal. She refused his favour and compassion. But how could she evade the well-deserved appeal for compassion.

A voice from inside Minu spoke, "Many girls have arrived here over the years. They beseeched all who mattered to let them go. But Minu had never interfered. This brothel no doubt is an exhibition of nudity. But since it was there, a hapless Minu could take refuge here. Like her, many unfortunate girls reached here seeking shelter. They have taken refuge on their own. The idea to release Arundhati was an effort to rip it to pieces. If Minu had anything to do with such a plan, she would be accused of breach of trust. The one who supported the consumer could never side with the consumed. Such thought was unethical and such act could be construed as treacherous.

However, Arundhati addressed her as 'Maa'. She held her feet and beseeched her to help her out. How could she evade the call of her heart? Could she have done so if Arundhati were her own daughter? Wouldn't she have put to use her wisdom and energy to set her free from the dark room?

Minu grew firm. She was not only Minu, she was not only a whore, she was not only someone's daughter or daughter-in-law. Enough that she was a woman. She was related to Arundhati that way. She cannot tolerate another woman losing her everything and living her life as a whore. She wouldn't allow another unfortunate woman rotting in the dark dungeons of prostitution.

Where would she hide Arundhati, evading the watchful eyes of Badadei, the hired goons of Munsif Mian, the pimps and other such people? If she even made an attempt to escape during the day, she would be easily detected by them. At night, there was quite a crowd, preventing any such possibility. Minu was unable to plan out a suitable time to carry out her mission.

She looked outside through the railings on the window. Just behind the brothel, there ran a narrow drain carrying the water with unbearable stench. Broken glass bottles, eggshells, discarded cotton and empty cigarette packets lay scattered. Filled with air, a discarded condom flew like a balloon, displaying someone's timid manhood. Thorny plants grew in abundance some distance away. Next to these, there was the barbed-wire fence. A narrow footpath lay beyond. There was a faint possibility of taking this path to escape.

She opened the door and came to the verandah. At sight of Param Mondal and Munsif Mian, she retreated inside immediately. Munsif Mian soon knocked on her door.

A stream of sweat ran down Minu's body. She had not met him for days. He looked terrible. On his perfectly tidy and ironed Punjabi lay a gold chain up to the navel. He was wearing Nagra shoes. Param Mondal followed him.

"What's up?"

Munsif Mian asked Minu. His eyes glistened like the eyes of a fox at night. Minu grew dreadful for a moment. Had Munsif Mian any clues to what she had in her mind?

She swallowed spittle and said, "All fine, Sir."

Munsif Mian continued, "This room is fine. Shift to the other room for a day. The new 'item' will be put up here. What do you say, Param?"

Param Mondal bowed down to say 'yes'. He gazed here and there through the room and said, "Yes, this room is better."

"Yes. You have to shift for some time. Badadei will explain everything. Let me go now." Munsif Mian left soon.

After their departure, Minu returned to the room and sat on her bed for some time. How terrible these people are ! They have a vigilant eye on Arundhati. The person who was supposed to arrive the next day, was already keeping a watch. She was drenched in sweat by then. She went near the window and stood there for some time.

Munsif Mian had asked her to vacate the room. This room was comparatively more spacious than other rooms. Minu took great care to keep it tidy. Her days in this room were numbered now. One day in the past, someone else must have vacated this room to make place for her. She was in great demand then. She had lost favour with the customers. The new 'item' was going to be the new sensation. She was supposed to bring more money for Munsif.

At the thought of vacating the room, Minu felt decimated inside. She felt as if she wasn't vacating the room but rather the room was expelling her. She had lost her status to occupy the room anymore.

There was a time when she thought that the room belonged to her. It was her own. The bed, the cupboard, photos of the deities, electric bulbs, and the old fan—everything belonged to her. She would stay there till death in their company. However, she had never thought that she would lose her worth and turn useless so early. Such thoughts now were sure to distress her.

This was the room in which she had presented herself copious tears and sobs. She had banged her head many times blaming her ill-fate. Her innumerable unfulfilled desires and dreams resided in this room. How could she vacate it?

Minu could never share her feelings with anyone. No one would be interested in this too. She readied herself mentally to vacate the room. If needed, she would vacate the brothel. But, she must do her best to release Arundhati.

Minu got up. Nabaghan was going downstairs through the verandah. She called out to him, "Nabaghan ! Please come here."

Nabaghan had already crossed Minu's door. While taking a few steps back, he said, "Minudei, I'm coming."

"Are you going to the market," Minu asked.

"Yes, tell me if you need something."

Minu looked here and there and said, "Buy a notebook and a pen for me. Take this five rupee note."

Nabaghana looked at Minu, surprised. He always found it difficult to comprehend her. He said, "Minudei, do you want to rejoin your studies?"

Minu remained mum. What was the use of studies anymore? Did whatever education she had acquired came in use in her life? Why should she waste her time at this age? She told him, "You go now. I need a notebook to keep accounts. I need one for that."

Nabaghana left for the market.

Arundhati had a fresh lease of life at the sight of Minu. She had been kept confined like a cow in a barred cowshed. Within a week, she had exhausted her reservoir of tears. She neither ate nor drank anything. She didn't feel like listening to anyone. Although, initially she was unaware of why she had been brought here, she now had ample ideas. Fear and terror seized her at times. She would shiver violently at times.

From whatever discussions Minu had with Arundhati, she could clearly guess about the latter's village and home. Her village was close to a railway station. From a distance, it looked like a mole on a face. At the middle of the village stood Arundhati's house. Made of raw bricks and mud, her house had a thatched roof. Pumpkin and gourd creepers spread everywhere on the roof. Her mother had drawn *jhoti* designs on the walls on the occasion of *Manabasa Gurubara*. Arundhati drew flowers and creepers on those designs. With the prints of her fingers, she had drawn designs of the overflowing *mana*. At the sight of her designs, her proud parents often expressed great delight.

That day, Arundhati had left home before ten o'clock. At the foot of the sacred tulsi plant, at the threshold of the puja room and at the Mangala temple, she had prayed the deities beseeching them to grant her success in finding a job. If that happened, she would be able to dispel sorrows from the life of her parents.

Instead of dispelling their sorrows she had rather multiplied them. What would her father be doing now? Like a mad man, he would be running from one village to another, from one police station to another. Her mother would have become bed-ridden. Her younger brother would be watching them helplessly. Arundhati's sobs refused to accept any restraints. She broke into a violent wailing. How much sorrow and torture was ordained by God !

Minu patiently heard what she had to say. Then she spoke: "Control yourself. Don't worry. I'm there. Everything will be set right."

Just as a drowning man clutches at a straw, Arundhati inched closer to Minu and held her tightly.

Minu fingered through Arundhati's dishevelled hair. She planted kisses on her tear-moistened eyes. She fondly caressed her back, hands, nose and ears. She nailed through her hair in a manner of combing it.

Minu advised, "Listen to me carefully. Don't tell anyone that you had reached this brothel. Others will get an opportunity to despise you. Tell them anything else that you wish but don't take the name of the brothel."

Arundhati's timid appearance brightened up at the prospect of getting respite from the place. Minu closed the door, took her to the window on the west and made her sit on the bed. She started combing Arundhati's hair. She felt as if God had really blessed her with a child. She had become a real mother. All her dreams got fulfilled.

Minu was reminded of her mother. She remembered how she felt restless when Minu insisted on going to the rehearsal hall to practice dance. She would be angry with her. However, at night after Minu fell asleep, her mother would caress her hair. She would anoint her feet with oil. She would address her as 'my sweet child, my loving child,' plant kisses on her cheeks and cover her with a shawl. Minu could visualize her fair and perked up figure smeared with turmeric paste. She had never visualized her figure so distinctly earlier. Emotional Minu held Arundhati in her lap and said, "I'll give you freedom from here. My daughter will never become a whore. My daughter will not die a death every day of her life.'

But, the question was how to grant freedom from this fort? For the last three days, she had been making one plan after another, although without much success. Munsif Mian was supposed to come in the evening. Before the beast arrived, she had to release Arundhati from the hell. If Arundhati didn't escape today, she would never be able to escape. Her life would lose its meaning.

Arundhati was listening to Minu with interest. Minu had been making one plan after another just to ensure that Arundhati escaped and reached Pranakrushna in the police station. Only in that case, she could reach her village. Pranakrushna was her last resort. She knew he would surely help her. But, if he was absent for some reason, what would she do? The police officials were hand in gloves with Munsif Mian. They might inform him about her escape. If that happened, Arundhati would be brought back to the hell to rot forever.

Things shouldn't take such a turn. Minu prayed to God. She had written a letter addressed to Pranakrushna the previous night. She had beseeched him to personally take Arundhati to her village and drop her with her parents.

She had comforted Arundhati many times too. She had coaxed and cajoled her. "You have taken birth as a woman. A woman has to hold on to someone's fingers for support. It mayn't be difficult to leave the support, but it would be difficult to get fresh support. A woman's life is much like a glass tumbler. If dealt carelessly, it gets shattered into pieces. Then, it'll be difficult to manage her world."

"This society belongs to men. They have shaped it for their own use. Here, a woman is much like a flower vase or a doormat. That's why you have to depend on someone throughout your life. You have to seek the support of your father, brother or husband." It was not true that Arundhati didn't understand such things. She understood everything explicitly and was full of remorse. She even vowed never to be befooled by false promises and venture out again.

Minu would suppress her anger and ponder how she could help her escape.

Someone was knocking at the door. Minu felt enraged. She was hardly allowed a moment of privacy. While going towards the door to open it, she told Arundhati, "Wait. Let me go and find out who it is."

Minu closed the door and came outside. Chandrakala was standing on the verandah. Irritated, Minu asked, "What happened?"

"Badadei has sent this. Take this and help her to put on." Without waiting for Minu's reaction, Chandrakala placed a packet in her hands and disappeared. Minu felt as if she received an electric shock. She realized, the time was drawing near. She had a couple of hours at hand. After that, there'll be no need of thinking or planning anything.

She flung the packet on to the bed and stood near the staircase. Then, instead of running downstairs, she ran upstairs to the roof.

The sea looked clear from there. The tall coconut

trees and roofs of tall buildings were distinctly visible too. It was evening. The street lights were about to be switched on. Minu's heart throbbed with rapid pulsation. She was afraid. Earlier, she had displayed courage only for her sake. But today, she wasn't concerned about herself. She had already become old. On the other hand, Arundhati was only a child, she had a long future.

She was reminded of Nabaghana once again. He was effeminate, no doubt, but he had a kind heart. He knew Pranakrushna quite well. Only he could guide Arundhati to Pranakrushna. Otherwise, it would be like jumping from the frying pan into the fire. If Arundhati failed to reach her parents safely, all her efforts would go in vain.

At the dream of success, Minu felt light in her heart. She came down. Only a few people were roaming around. The vendor at the sweets shop was lighting the hearth. Shutting the door and windows tight, she beckoned Arundhati, "Come."

As if in a trance, Arundhati got up. Minu said, "Take off these clothes. No…no…wait. Let me put on this new saree first."

Minu unwrapped the packet. It contained a new saree, a new blouse and a new petticoat. Minu wrapped herself in the new saree only. She put the blouse and petticoat back into the packet and threw it under the bed.

"It's all right now. Put on my clothes. Quick. We don't have much time to spare."

Arundhati hardly understood the reason behind the change of clothes. She gazed at Minu, wide-eyed.

Minu said, "The new saree had been sent for you. Munsif Mian had sent it. Hmm !" Minu's face contracted in disdain.

Arundhati had already put on Minu's clothes. Minu

took her to the window and said, "Look, I'll help you cross the railing. With the help of the knots on the saree, go down. Run straight. You'll find a postbox. To the right of that, there's the police station. Pranakrushna babu is the inspector there. Hand over this letter to him. Do you understand?"

Arundhati nodded her head and said, "And what about you?"

Minu sighed deeply and said, "Where can I go, from here? I have already crossed forty. How long am I supposed to live? I can spend the rest of my life here. Leave it. There's no time to discuss this. Remember, don't give up courage. I pray God, if He wills you'll reach your parents soon."

Arundhati's eyes welled up. She realized, Minu would sit on the bed in her place. She'll have to pay a price for her freedom. In order to satisfy the hunger of the dreadful, she'll give herself up at their feet.

She wished to stay back a little and have deeper knowledge about this lady. She would listen to her story as to why a Goddess like woman spent a vicious life here in the brothel. Was it to redeem some curse or for the relief of unfortunate people like her?

Minu, in the meantime, had removed a few screws with a screwdriver and removed a part of the railing. She tied a few knots on two sarees and hung them from there. "Beware ! Don't ever try to take the road at front. Someone will surely find you there. Take the road at the back. About ten steps beyond the guava tree, there is a road."

Arundhati nodded in agreement.

Minu said, "Let me go and inform Nabaghana. Shut the door from inside."

Arundhati switched off the light and sat enveloped in darkness. Each moment passed like an aeon. She made a mental note of the route and the plan that Minu had discussed with her. She had to get down at the back. There was a footpath by the guava tree. The footpath ran ahead, turned to the left some distance away and touched the main road. She had to go straight till the post box. To the right of the post box stood the police station. She had to go in and hand over the letter to Pranakrushna babu there.

She picked up the letter lying on the blanket and placed it inside her blouse. She was drenched in sweat. Dread and excitement made her restless.

Minu returned and sat on the bed. Arundhati shut the door from inside and said, "What happened?"

"Nabaghana is absent. Someone has sent her on some errand. I don't know what to do."

Arundhati replied, "Don't you worry at all, Maa. I can manage alone. I have your blessings."

Blessings ! What blessings can a whore shower? Minu gazed at Arundhati. Had she been a mother, she would have dressed her in a new saree. She would have applied powder and anointed her with oil. But she had put on Arundhati's new saree herself and asked her to put on her old clothes. Wasn't it a mockery of justice?

She got up. She pulled out the trunk from under the bed and took out a small packet. In it, she had a few notes, a nose-ring and a ring. She tied these in a handkerchief. She tucked it into Arundhati's dress and said, "Keep this. I don't have anything worthier than this. It'll surely come handy. If by chance Pranakrushna babu is absent, hand these along with the letter over to the official you find there. Have you carried the letter with you?"

"Yes."

"Tell him, 'Sir...take this stuff but take me to my parents.'"

Minu's voice was choking. Tear streamed down her cheeks. Was it out of joy or sorrow? She didn't know. She clasped Arundhati once again and planted kisses all on her lips, cheeks and forehead. She went to the photos of the deities, brought a little sandalwood paste and applied it on Arundhati's forehead. She took her to the window and said, "Now leave. Don't lose hope or be afraid. You have my blessings. You also carry God's grace. I'm sure you'll reach your destination without trouble."

Arundhati turned back. She bent down to touch Minu's feet. This was an emotional moment-- a moment to disappear soon like smoke. She tried her best to restrain her tears. This was not the moment to shed tears. There'll be many such moments in future, for sure.

Arundhati climbed down through the window just as Minu had instructed her. Minu was left whispering, "Careful…careful…"

The moon had hidden under a patch of cloud. Minu felt as if God lent support to what she was doing. He had deliberately dimmed the heavenly light. Arundhati reached the ground. Her feet touched it. Minu waved frantically to her, "Go…go…run away." She disappeared soon from the spot.

After Arundhati's complete disappearance, Minu breathed easy. She ran to the bed and sat on it. Her heart was pulsating heavily. Her feet and hands were sweating profusely in dread. Her entire body had sweated once like this on the day she had run away from Kalapat village. However, today she wasn't at all concerned about herself. She had only one concern—Arundhati must reach her destination safely. If she was apprehended on the way, that would mean disaster for Minu no doubt, but it would also mean end of the road for Arundhati.

Minu prayed,"O God ! Please guide the child safely to her parents. I'll offer you milk and coconuts in *bhog*. Please lend her support."

"Open the door, my queen, open the door."

"Who is it?" Minu was about to shout loudly. She restrained her on the realization that she wasn't Minu but Arundhati. Minu had gone out somewhere. She was left alone at home. She was around seventeen or eighteen.

The knock was repeated. Minu was deliberately delaying to open the door. The more time she took, the more she would be assured of Arundhati's safety. Besides, Minu felt satiated to see men crave for pleasure. She derived cruel pleasure to make them impatient and restive. How many unfortunate women were exploited by their cruel husbands every day ! They dry their tears in the fire of the hearths just for few pieces of sarees and two square meals a day.

An enraged Munsif Mian yelled loudly, "Open the door, it's me."

The entire room was steeped in darkness. She had switched off the lights long ago. Minu gathered courage, reached the door and opened it.

Munsif Mian wasn't alone. There was someone else giving him company. Minu couldn't recognize him in the pervading darkness. Arundhati was tall and thin. On the other hand, a layer of fat had accumulated around Minu's waist. She looked obese. What if he perceived the difference !

Munsif Mian closed the door. Strong odour of foreign liquor emanated from his mouth and spread everywhere. The tuberose garlands failed to dispel the odour. He wobbled and also spoke incoherently. Minu swallowed some spittle and sat on the bed.

"Why have you got the room dark, dear? Will the

dazzle of the light fade in comparison to your beauty? What do you say?" Munsif roared loudly.

Minu didn't seek the light for obvious reasons. She protested, "No…no…let the room be dark.'

"Okay…okay…whatever you wish." Munsif Mian came closer. Minu knew quite well what would happen then. Whenever a new girl reached the brothel, Munsif enjoyed her flesh first. He had absolute monopoly in this regard.

Forget about love, Minu didn't harbour the slightest appreciation for Munsif. She treated him with contempt. She had mentally prepared herself for any consequence.

Like a hunting dog, Munsif Mian sprang upon her. His paws were crushing her shoulders. Minu suppressed her breathing and endured the pain.

Suddenly, Munsif Mian loosened the grip of his paws from her bosom and waist. Minu failed to decipher what had prompted him to do so. She grew terrified. He dragged his feet towards the switch board, groped for it in the dark and pressed the switch. The room soon was flooded in bright light.

Minu stood in one corner, her palms covering her face. The new saree had slipped from her waist and was lying on the ground.

"You bloody bitch. How dare you betray me like this ! Duplicity with Munsif Mian ! It will cost you dear."

Munsif Mian yelled. The heart of the faded yellow building shivered. Minu retreated a couple of steps. Sexual arousal coupled with annoyance at being betrayed made Munsif Mian's body shiver. His eyes glistened like the eyes of a wounded wolf. He hollered, "Param, you bloody bastard…come here."

Param Mondal was roaming on the verandah. If Munsif was satisfied, he might kindly offer him a commission. It was no mean a task to convince Arundhati to come with him. Besides, the way he hoodwinked the policemen and T.T.Es of the railways, he certainly deserved a hike in commission.

He never expected that Munsif Mian would holler like this. He pushed open the door and rushed inside.

"This bloody whore has debauched me. Ask her where she has kept my new 'item' hidden."

Param Mondal had by now witnessed the condition of the unfortunate railing. He ran towards the railing and pulled the saree tied to it as if expecting that Arundhati would be hanging from the other end.

Sad and fearful, Minu's heart was pounding at the prospect of being caught.

In a moment, Munsif Mian realized what had transpired. He at once understood that Minu had conspired to get him arrested by the police. She had already cast a net for the purpose. Crazy in anger and excitement, he fished out a spring knife from his kurta pocket. In the twinkle of an eye, the sharp point of the angry weapon disappeared into her abdomen and came out stained in red horror.

Param Mondal's eyes closed of their own.

Pressing the wounded abdomen with her hands, Minu cried out horrendously and collapsed on the pool of her own blood.

Munsif Mian and Param Mandal were seen fleeing through the open door. The blood-stained knife lay on the floor.

Intense pain permeated through Minu's entire body. She felt as if her abdomen was split open. However, amidst such pain Minu felt relaxed at heart. She was happy with what she had done. She had done what was right. How could she have allowed her daughter to be a whore?

She realized her time was running out. No one would shed tears at her death. Like a dog being run over by a truck, she was going to die far away from her near and dear ones.

The pain in the abdomen was unbearable. It had permeated to her hands, feet, chest and head. She felt as if she was Arundhati's real mother. How could a mother bear a child without shedding blood?

Minu felt as if someone was playing kettledrums and *mridanga* nearby. The sound resembled the sound those instruments produced when Gangadhar Sir was playing them. The instruments were producing loud music. Perhaps the player had gone mad.

The brothel was alarmed at the blaring of the sirens by the police jeep. No one expected police to arrive at such an odd hour. People ran, helter-skelter, putting on anything that they could lay their hands on.

Pranakrushna and Arundhati, followed by two constables, descended on Minu's door. Arundhati ran ahead and showed them the way, "Here."

The door was left wide open. Pranakrushna, while entering inside, suddenly halted.

Arundhati called out loudly, "Maa…Maa !"

Pranakrushna was gazing at the stream of blood that had run till the threshold. Minu's blood-soaked body was lying in front. He ran and picked up Minu's left hand. After some time, he put it back on the ground and got up.

Setting aside her patience, dismay and dread, Arundhati suddenly cried out in distress. Her shout pierced through the heart of the dark night and shattered its silence.

❑❑

Glossary

Amavasya:	The new moon night
Babu:	A Hindu title of address equivalent to Sir or Mr.
Badichura:	Sun dried lentil dumpling and coarse mixture of onion, garlic, green chillies, mustard oil etc.
Batiskala Sadhaka:	An exorcist who is highly experienced
Bhai:	Brother
Bhog:	Food offered to a deity
Biri:	A cheap form of cigarette made from cut tobacco rolled in a leaf
Chaturdashi:	An auspicious day in the Hindu calendar
Chita and Jhoti:	Designs drawn on the walls using rice paste
Dadan:	Poor migrants migrating to other states to work
Dalmankudi:	A folk game that children play by moving from one branch to the other.
Dei:	A reverential way of addressing an elder sister
Dhaba:	A local restaurant
Dhol:	A type of drum
Dolapurnami:	Full moon day in the month of Phalguna, the eleventh month of the Hindu calendar
Ekadasi:	Eleventh day of the Hindu lunar calendar
Gamchha:	A traditional thin, coarse cotton towel
Ghungroos:	Anklet bells
Gunth:	Approximately 1089 square feet

Jyestha:	Associated with high summer. Corresponds to May-June
Kajal:	A mixture of black powder and castor oil, used as a cosmetic
Kaudi khela:	game with kauri shells
Kendu:	Diospyros melanoxylon, a tree native to India and Sri lanka
Krishnachura:	Delonix regia remarkable for its orange-red flowers over Summer
Krishnapaksha:	A term used in the Hindu calendar to refer to the second fortnight of the lunar month in which the moon is fading
Ladoo:	A sphere shaped sweet made from flour, ghee and sugar
Mahadeepa:	The huge lamp burnt atop Hindu temples on special occasions
Mana:	A measuring unit used in the past
Manabasa Gurubara:	Observed by Odias in the month of Margasira, the ninth month of the Hindu calendar
Mridanga:	A drum used in India and shaped like an elongated barrel
Pakhala:	Freshly cooked rice soaked in water and fermented overnight
Pakoda:	Spiced fritter sold by street vendors and restaurants
Palamandap:	A community place where palas are held. Papas are a performing art from the Indian state of Odisha
Pana Sankranti:	Also known as Maha Vishuba Sankranti, Traditional New Year Day in Odisha

Rath yatra: Chariot festival of Lord Jagannath, Puri
Sahada tree: Streblus asper
Samosa: A fried or baked pastry with a savory filling such as spiced potato, peas etc.
Saradhabali: The bank of Malini River filled with sand in Puri, the Holly town in Odisha
Shravan: Fifth month of the Hindu calendar
Solakala Sadhaka: An experienced exorcist
Srimandir: The abode of Lord Jagannath, Balabhadra and goddess Subhadra and Laxmi
Treta yuga: Sanskrit name given to the second of the four Yugas in the Hindu myth.

Black Eagle Books

www.blackeaglebooks.org
info@blackeaglebooks.org

Black Eagle Books, an independent publisher, was founded
as a nonprofit organization in April, 2019. It is our mission
to connect and engage the Indian diaspora and the world at
large with the best of works of world literature published
on a collaborative platform, with special emphasis on
foregrounding Contemporary Classics and New Writing.